## Payback

"…a great book. You'll cry a lot. You'll smile a few times. You might even chuckle a bit. In the end, you'll be glad you read it."
—On Top Down Under Reviews

"I do love my humorous, quirky John Inman books but this serious side of him grips me just as much. In fact this one has just shot way high into my favourite John reads."
—Sinfully… Addicted to All Male Romance

"I really enjoyed this… The story is well written and gripping from the start, and kept my attention throughout its sadly poetic storyline."
—MM Good Book Reviews

## Head-on

"Brilliant, evocative, poignant, heartrending… It will force you to tackle an ethical dilemma. It will ask you to judge and forgive. But it will also make your heart sing. And give you hope."
—My Fiction Nook

## Spirit

"It was sweet! Not sappy sweet, though… Just two sexy guys falling in love during the middle of a pretty intense situation."
—The Blogger Girls

"…a good book, and an entertaining story…"
—Love Bytes

By JOHN INMAN

Chasing the Swallows
A Hard Winter Rain
Head-on
Hobbled
Jasper's Mountain
Loving Hector
Paulie
Payback
The Poodle Apocalypse
Shy
Snow on the Roof (Dreamspinner Anthology)
Spirit

THE BELLADONNA ARMS
Serenading Stanley
Work in Progress

Published by DREAMSPINNER PRESS
http://www.dreamspinnerpress.com

# Chasing the
# Swallows

JOHN INMAN

Published by
DREAMSPINNER PRESS

5032 Capital Circle SW, Suite 2, PMB# 279, Tallahassee, FL 32305-7886 USA
http://www.dreamspinnerpress.com/

Chasing the Swallows
© 2015 John Inman.

Cover Art
© 2015 Maria Fanning.
Cover content is for illustrative purposes only and any person depicted on the cover is a model.

ISBN: 978-1-63216-917-4
Digital ISBN: 978-1-63216-918-1
Library of Congress Control Number: 2014922531
First Edition April 2015

Printed in the United States of America
∞
This paper meets the requirements of
ANSI/NISO Z39.48-1992 (Permanence of Paper).

*For John B.*

# Chapter One

WHEN I answered the door, checkbook in hand, the fantasy washed over me like a wave of warm water. My God…

*…THE BUG man was cute. Maybe twenty years old, tops. He had short blond hair under a baseball cap tilted to the back of his head and the pale complexion of a Nordic god. He displayed a pretty nice lump of what I assumed was man meat bulging out the fly of his white bug-man pants, which I must say was what had grabbed my attention in the first place.*

*Being concerned with pests, as bug men usually are, he stared at me like I had just popped out of a gopher hole.*

*"What did you say?" he asked, still holding his bug-spraying apparatus and looking like maybe he was employing a great deal of restraint in an effort not to use it on me.*

*I cleared my throat and tried again. "I said, why don't you come inside and relax for a while. Get out of the sun."*

*"Get out of the sun." He echoed my words with little to no inflection. He looked down at the bug sprayer in his hand, then back to me. "And you'll give me a hundred-dollar bill?"*

*I dusted off my best smile. "Brand spanking new."*

*He glanced at his watch, then back to the bug sprayer, then back to me. "And all you want to do is suck my dick."*

*I nodded. The young man understood after all. "Until you come. Yeah. What do you say?"*

*He wiggled his nose and blinked three times like Elizabeth Montgomery, gazed back over his shoulder at his truck with the big plastic bug sitting on the roof, then down at his watch, then down at the bug sprayer, and then back to me.*

*"Are you crazy?" he asked.*

1

*"Probably," I said.*

*He looked up at the sun, then back to the truck, then at his watch, then down to the bug sprayer, then back to me. Jesus. I was getting a crick in my neck watching him.*

*"Make it two hundred," he said.*

*I gnawed on that for a second. I wasn't really as desperate as all that, was I?*

*Guess so. With a new sense of respect for my adversary, I fished in my pocket and dug out two one-hundred-dollar bills. I snapped them crisply in front of my face for the lad's benefit and stepped back from the door so he could come inside. No pun intended.*

*"Leave your bug sprayer on the porch," I said.*

*So he did.*

*He stepped into my living room, tilted his hat a little farther back on his head, and watched me with an odd smirk on his face as I dropped to my knees in front of him (all the while trying not to grunt—damned arthritis!) and began undoing his belt buckle and working down the zipper on his trousers. Unless I was hallucinating from dementia, which wouldn't have surprised me in the least, the lad was getting a hard-on inside his bug-man trousers, and that hard-on was looking quite fetching. Yes indeedy.*

*"Are you queer?" he asked, watching me.*

*"Congratulations," I said. "You just won the bonus round for asking the dumbest question ever."*

*"Wow," he said. "What do I get for that?"*

*"Nothing."*

*With his belt undone and his zipper unzipped, I plucked the snap at the top of his trousers and let gravity take over. His oversized white bug-man pants poured down his legs like a bank of snow sliding off a roof. Being a lad after my own heart, he wasn't wearing any undies, so once the pants slid away, his lovely young cock sprang up and bonked me on the nose.*

2

*"Ooh," I said. He might not be the brightest bulb in the chandelier, but when you have youth and beauty on your side, what does that matter?*

*I cradled his cock in my hand and gave it a stroke or two just to be friendly. Before I slurped the head of it into my mouth like a big fat strawberry off an ice cream sundae, I looked up into his eyes and asked, "You don't have termites or anything, do you?"*

*It took him a moment to come to grips with that question. I'm not sure if it was outside his learning curve to realize I was joking or if the fact that I was holding on to his pecker had short-circuited his question-answering capabilities.*

*"I don't think so," he finally said.*

*I considered that response. "Well, you're a bug man, after all. If you had termites, you'd probably know it."*

*That cheered him up. "I guess I would."*

*He took a teeny step forward and pressed his dick to my lips. "Best get on with it," he said. "I've got ants on Fern Street to see to. Mrs. Harbuckle was kind of panicky. She hates ants."*

*"You bet," I said. "Poor woman."*

*I slid my mouth over his cock and sucked it in until his blond pubic hair was tickling my nose. His legs started to shake. He grabbed the back of my head like he was about to go two-handed bowling, and gave my mouth a couple of pumps with his hips.*

*"Holy moly," he gasped. "That feels dandy."*

*I nodded, too preoccupied to speak. Grabbing his pale young ass with both hands and pulling him closer, I tried to get his balls into my mouth too. Didn't quite work. He must have been appreciative of my effort, at least, for at that very moment, he tensed every muscle in his body, rose up onto his tippy toes like a ballerina, and dumped about a quart of hot jism down my throat. It was all I could do to keep up with the flow without donning water wings so I wouldn't drown.*

*Just when I thought the young man was finished, he grabbed my head one more time, gave his ass a quick shimmy with his cock still down my throat, and coughed up another squirt of come. Just a little one. Sort of a delicious afterthought.*

*He trembled for about five seconds, slowly slid his softening dick from between my lips, and reached down into my shirt pocket to pluck out the two hundred-dollar bills I had stashed there.*

*"I'd best finish squirting your aphids now, sir," he said, pulling his pants up.*

*I nodded and, still on my knees, waited as he straightened his bug-man uniform. He tucked his dick and shirt discreetly into his baggy white pants, and slipped the money in too. Whistling a merry tune, he sang out, "Later, Mr. Ayres," as he stepped out into the sunlight on wobbly legs and closed my front door behind him....*

I FINISHED writing the check and handed it to Stephen through the screen door because I didn't want Sylvester to get out. Sylvester was our cat.

Stephen, the bug man, doffed his hat and said, "Thank you, Mr. Ayres. Hope Arthur's feeling better."

I smiled and stepped out onto the porch, carefully closing the door behind me as I kept an eye out for Sylvester, who was quicker than a snake when he had an agenda. "He's fine, thank you, Stephen. I told him not to run that marathon, but he wouldn't listen. Now he's bed bound with a pulled muscle in his gluteus maximus."

"His what?"

"His ass. How's your young wife?"

Stephen blushed. "She's fine, sir. Thanks. She told me not to forget to say thanks for the cookies you gave us last time I was here."

"Liked them, did she?"

"Yeah. She asked me to ask for the recipe."

"Tell her I'll leave it to her in my will."

He perked up. "Really?"

"No."

Stephen grinned. "That's what I thought. Oh, well, you guys'll probably outlive Sharon and me anyway. Well, I'd best be off. Gotta swarm of bees to run off three streets over."

I tsked. "Well, don't let 'em get you."

"I'll run like a rabbit if they get too close."

We both had a good laugh over that, mine more sincere than his, and I gave him a final wave as he drove off in the big white bug-man truck with the big plastic bug on the roof.

I clucked my tongue as his truck turned onto Jasper Street, one block up, and disappeared.

God, that boy was gorgeous.

I sighed and wandered back to the house after plucking a dandelion out of the yard by the front steps. When I reached out for the doorknob to let myself back into the house and saw Arthur standing behind the screen, I jumped about two feet straight up into the air. He was still in his pajamas, and the day was almost over.

"You startled me," I said. Before turning the doorknob, I asked, "Where's the cat?"

Arthur gave a good-natured grunt. "You mean Houdini, the escape artist? He's nowhere near. Come on in."

So I did.

Arthur's hair was sticking out on both sides of his head like Bozo the clown's, only not exactly red. His was in the salt and cinnamon stage, where redheads often go when they start to gray. My own hair was simply salt. No, we are not young. Neither of us. In fact, we had been lovers for a longer period of time than most people have been alive on the planet. Our fortieth anniversary would be upon us before we knew it, but neither one of us had talked about it much. After thirty-nine of the damn things, one more didn't seem like that big a deal.

I had noticed of late that Arthur's British accent was now so faint as to be almost undetectable. It was a far cry from the delectable British lilt his voice had carried almost four decades earlier when he was new to this country—and even newer to me. Somehow his voice had softened over the years. Now his words rolled off his tongue sounding complacent and homey and as comforting as warm milk. I wasn't sure why that had begun to annoy me so much. I supposed I missed the shivers of delight the crisp enunciation of his youth had sent through me way back when. Back when love was an adventure, not a heart-numbing grind.

"How you feeling?" I asked, trying to swallow a sigh.

"Like a side of pickled pig's feet nobody ordered."

"What's that supposed to mean?"

He chuckled, then groaned and grabbed his hip when he turned to walk toward his recliner in the corner. "Davey, you know exactly what I mean. You couldn't look any hungrier for that boy if you carried a knife and fork and wore a napkin around your neck."

"I don't know what you're talking about."

He eased himself into his chair, said a soft "Ouch" when his injured ass hit the cushion, then grinned up at me in total disbelief. "Oh, please. When he's within a mile and a half, you don't even know my name. I think maybe you import bugs from the neighbors just to have an excuse to ask him over here."

It was my turn to say, "Oh, please." Then I bent down with one hand at the small of my back like an obsequious waiter and handed Arthur the dandelion I had plucked from the yard. "For you," I said. "Now shut the hell up."

To my surprise, he blushed.

"And don't do any more marathons, Arthur. You're too old."

"Fuck you."

"That's mature."

He eyeballed me long enough to make me squirm. I hate it when he does that. His voice was pure ice water. "Stop fantasizing about the bug man. I'm right here. Fantasize about me."

I narrowed my eyes and went "Pfft."

"What the hell is *that* supposed to mean?" he asked.

"It means I don't need to fantasize about what I already have."

"Would you like me to arrange it so you don't have it any more?"

"Are you threatening to leave?"

He sniffed the fucking dandelion. "Maybe."

I spread my arms wide and executed what I imagined to be a perfect pirouette, although I have to admit it probably wasn't perfect at all. The ever-recurring glitch in my knee prevented perfection, you see. Old age sucks. It really does. "How can you leave? We own all this together. House, lot, cars, cat, too much furniture, the whole shebang. We're stuck."

He rolled his eyes. "That's a romantic way to put it."

"And I wasn't fantasizing about the bug man." It was a lie, and I knew it. Hopefully, he didn't. That hope, of course, didn't exactly pan out.

He rolled his eyes *again*. "You fantasize about the bug man, the cable guy, the gardener, the priest at the fucking church, and you're *still* fantasizing about the Vietnamese guy who dug up the hibiscus bushes three years ago."

I took an untimely stroll down memory lane. "God, now *there* was a hunk."

"Asshat," Arthur groused, dropping the footrest on his recliner with a thud. He wrestled himself to his feet and would have stormed out of the room in a red-hot minute if he could have mustered that much speed. As it was, he simply ambled, and rather unsteadily at that, but I must admit he made his exit with singularity of purpose. He was obviously pissed.

"You really shouldn't be running any more marathons!" I bellowed after him. "I'll get your medicine and bring it to you."

"Don't bother!" he shot back. "Go stand by the front window and wait for your jogger to show up like you do every other day of the fucking year!"

"Oh, don't be silly," I said. And the moment Arthur slammed the bedroom door behind him, I hurried to the picture window overlooking the street and waited for the high point of my day to go past.

I called him Dennis, although I had no idea in the world what his name really was.

The sun was warm on my face as I stood at the glass peering out. One of my neighbors, Miss Johannsen, strolled past with her pair of Weimaraners in tow. She spotted me in the window and waved hello. I waved back since it was already too late to step back into the shadows and avoid her completely.

A moment later my jogger, Dennis, topped the hill and came clomping his way toward the house, where, if he followed his usual path, he would turn left and proceed down the same road the bug man had taken a few minutes earlier.

I blinked into the noonday sunshine and suddenly my imagination was off and running on a merry path all its own…

THE PEPPER tree had been dead for a year. It was time to get rid of the fucker. Rather than hire a tree surgeon to do it, I decided to take care of the problem myself. It's not like I was risking life and limb by climbing into the heavens or anything. It was just a little tree, not standing more than six feet high.

It had roots, however, that must have reached all the way to Shanghai.

I dug out the ground around the base of the tree without much problem, but when the trunk still couldn't be induced to give me so much as a wiggle, I sawed it off to a two-foot stump, which, even without a tree atop it, was set in the ground firmly as a telephone pole.

I was grunting and cussing and sweating up a storm trying to make the damn thing weaken its grip on the earth when I heard thudding footsteps approach.

Standing with a groan, I turned to find Dennis the Jogger standing behind me, sweating as much as I was and looking absolutely stunning in a tiny pair of yellow running shorts that covered his dick and not much else. He stood there with his hands on his hips, his chest heaving as he dragged in oxygen to replace what he had expended during his run, eyeballing me and my tree with a happy glint in his eyes.

The eyes, by the way, were forest green. I had never been close enough to the man before to notice it.

I found myself sucked into those heavenly green eyes like a cup of coffee being absorbed by a dunked doughnut. And just like the doughnut, I ended up all mushy and soft. Well, not soft everywhere.

"Hi," I said.

"Hi back," he grinned. "Need some help, sir?"

I hated being called sir. Nothing makes an old guy feel older than a young guy calling him sir. But who was I to quibble? Dennis the Jogger could call me anything he wanted so long as he remained close enough for me to lose myself in those eyes and those teeny yellow running shorts.

"That's awfully kind of you, son. This tree is being a bit stubborn."

Dennis the Jogger grinned and shook his sweaty hair out of his eyes. He lifted both hands to push his hair away from his face, giving me a glimpse of two lovely armpits adorned with lovely clumps of hair. Even lovelier than the armpit hair was the view of his biceps as he held his arms aloft to let the air reach his forehead.

"I wasn't talking about the tree," he said. "I was talking about you watching me every time I run past. I was talking about the way your eyes never leave me until I'm out of sight over the crest of that hill over there." He pointed toward Jasper Street. "I'm talking about how maybe I'd like to let you fulfill your fantasy about me if you've still a mind to do it."

"M-my fantasy?"

He pointed to the rear of the house, back where the lawn met the canyon. Where the privacy was complete, and even neighborly eyes could not encroach.

"Let's go around the corner of the house for a minute, and I'll show you what I mean."

"I-I'm all sweaty." It was the only thing I could think of to say.

"So am I," Dennis the Jogger replied. "What are you afraid of?"

He reached out and took the shovel from my hand, flinging it aside. Then he reached out again and gripped my hand. With an innocent smile that made my heart thud like a jackhammer, he pulled me along the sidewalk to the back of the house, where the shade from the giant eucalyptus tree left us standing in a cool haven of shadow away from the broiling sun.

"No one can see us here, can they?" he asked.

I shook my head. "No."

"Not even your partner," he added.

"No," I agreed, glancing up at the second-floor window directly above us. That too was out of the line of sight for someone standing even directly in front of it. "No one can see us."

Dennis smiled and lowered me into a lawn chair at the base of the tree. He stepped in front of me and looked down at me gazing up at him. His chest was brown from the many hours he spent running shirtless. The wales of his ribs rippled down his sides, and his tiny belly button, with the tiny thatch of belly hair circling it, was less than ten inches from my nose.

He watched me staring at him. "Do you like what you see?" he asked.

It took me a heartbeat or two to find my voice. "Yes."

"Do you like my legs?" he asked.

I gazed at them. His legs were as brown as his chest and coated with a brushing of fine dark hair that I longed to press my face against. His quads were delineated, his calf muscles bulging from the run he had just interrupted. His knees were hard and trim and spare. I reached out to cup my hand behind each of them and felt the heat of his legs beneath the palms of my hands. Glancing up at his face, I saw him smile sweetly, as if about to bestow a gift. A moment later, still staring down at me, he hooked his thumbs in the waistband of his tiny yellow running shorts and slid them slowly off his hips. As they slid away, he first exposed a thatch of crisp brown pubic hair that almost crackled as it sprang up from the elastic dragging over it.

His hips moved to ease the downward movement of the running shorts, and suddenly the base of his cock was visible, nestled in the cloud of glistening pubic hair, looking comfy and soft and harmless.

"Let me," I muttered like a prayer, and he pulled his hands away to let me finish the job.

Hooking my own fingers into the waistband of his shorts, I pushed them down, away from the base of that peeking cock, and the minute the shorts slipped over the head of it, I let them fall to the ground at his feet.

Dennis the Jogger stood in front of me, his dick still nestled softly in its bed of pubes. He was uncircumcised, and his foreskin sheathed his cockhead, allowing only a glimpse of the wonder beneath.

I circled the cock with my fingertips and slid the foreskin back to expose the glans more fully. Dennis the Jogger took a step forward when I did.

I could smell the clean sweat on him now, and my salivary glands came to life. With my free hand, I cupped his heavy balls and felt the weight of them in my hand.

His cock began lengthening in my hand. His glans emerged from its sheath of foreskin and raised its head to peer at me. Dennis the Jogger reached out to cup my chin in his fingers, and as he held me securely, he took another step forward and laid his now erect cock against the side of my cheek.

I pressed my lips to his belly button and smiled as he did a slow dance of hunger with his cock against my face, sliding it first to one side of my nose, then to the other. The base of his penis smelled of sweat and youth and was the most erotic scent I had ever inhaled in my life.

As he continued to tease me with his cock, fully erect now and as hard and hot as sun-warmed marble, a gleam of *moisture began to exude from the opening at the tip. He smiled seeing it there and proceeded to smear the precome over my face from my eyes to my chin to my lips.*

*On his last pass across my lips, I opened myself up to him and let him slide his fat cockhead into my mouth and lay it gently atop my tongue. He took a tiny intake of breath when I closed my lips around it and drew it deeper into my mouth.*

*"Thank you," he muttered softly as his hips began to move, penetrating me deeper, then slowly pulling away until his cock was almost free of me, then sliding forward once again to bury himself in the wet satin heat of my mouth.*

*The air roiled up from the canyon behind us and cooled itself in the shade of the tree we were under. That same air dried the hair on Dennis the Jogger's body, and when it did, I ranged up and down his chest, his legs, the side of his neck, and all the way around to the small of his back with eager hands. When my fingertips brushed his spine, I tugged him gently into me until his young cock was buried as far as it would go in my eager, hungry mouth.*

*"Do you want my come?" he asked softly.*

*I nodded, opening my eyes to see his handsome face staring down, all the while still tasting the precome oozing deliciously from his cock.*

*He looked at me with an angelic fire in his eyes. He reached out gently to hold my head steady, and when I was no longer moving around him, he began sliding himself in and out of me.*

*"Easy," he whispered. "Easy."*

*I closed my eyes, lost in the eroticism of what was happening. His fingers slid gently over my ears, and he continued to hold my head still even as he stopped moving his cock in and out of my mouth. He stood for a moment, stock still, while his cock throbbed between my lips.*

*"Yes," he sighed, and his iron dick slowly slid from my mouth to rest atop my lips. The glans, swollen with blood, pressed to the side of my nose as I inhaled the scent of his hot balls pressing against my chin.*

*"Now," he moaned, and immediately his fingers buried themselves in my hair, and his slit spread wide to expunge a great gout of hot semen. The semen spilled out over my face and all the way up to my hairline. I clutched the back of his young, strong legs and opened my mouth wide to claim the last few drops of come still squirting from his cock.*

*He allowed me to claim it with a gasp and a tiny laugh, which made me smile.*

*As the last bit of come spilled from his body, blessing me with its sweetness and heat and sheer youthful beauty, he stroked the side of my face. He held his cock in place to soften slowly inside my mouth.*

*When at long last his cock slid free of my lips, I leaned forward in my chair and buried my come-splattered face in his stomach. He held me against him for a long moment as he stroked the back of my head, then he intoned a gentle, "Thank you."*

*With a sigh, as if he regretted what he was doing as much as I did, he stepped back, gave me a wink, and pulled his shorts up the long lovely stretch of his runner's legs to cover himself once again.*

*"Good-bye," he said with another wink, and a heartache later I could hear his thudding footsteps pounding the street away from my house toward the hill in the distance.*

*I blinked back a tear and glanced up at the second story window above my head.*

*There was no one in it gazing down. I wasn't sure if I was sorry or glad.*

I MET Arthur Smith at the Mission of San Juan Capistrano, just a little more than a stone's throw from the Pacific Ocean, on a balmy spring day in April, 1974. He was sitting all by himself on a stone bench within the garden walls of the mission. The rising sun spread golden arms of light around him as if he had been dropped there from the heavens—a new, young god evicted from the firmament above to bless the world below with his presence.

Lord, he was stunning.

He sat perched on the edge of that stone bench with his hands clasped peacefully in his lap, head tilted back to catch the rays of the morning sun, eyes closed, and a meditative smile smoothing his lips, as if his silent reverie was just beginning to enlighten him with the secrets of the universe.

I stood beneath an arbor of blossoming wisteria, the drone of bees in my ears, not breathing, brought to a furious, stunned stillness by the sight of the beautiful young man before me.

I was twenty-four, just out of college and finding my way in the world, at peace at last after finally accepting the truth about myself—the truth being that I was totally, unequivocally, and at long last unashamedly, gay. I had fought long and hard against that truth but eventually realized no matter how much I tore myself up, there was only one way for the battle to end.

Arthur Smith, I would learn on that long-ago spring morning of 1974, had never deigned to fight the same battle as I. He had merely embraced the fact that fate had declared him homosexual. After embracing it, he had moved on to the more important quest of seeking happiness in his life rather than facing the turmoil of refusing to accept who he really was, as I had done since the day puberty and all those new and frightening urges that accompany it had kicked me in the gut.

The final steps I would take down my long road to self-acceptance would be the short walk I made on that April morning along a flagstone path in the mission garden at San Juan Capistrano to ask the young god on the stone bench if I could join him in his reveries. Once I did ask, shyly, I never looked back. My acceptance of myself was complete. I would never forget the young god's reaction to my question.

He patted the stone bench beside him and said in a crisp British accent, the first I had actually heard in real life, "Please do. I saw you earlier and was hoping you would join me."

"Really?" I asked, standing before him, mesmerized by the melodic way his words rolled over me.

He didn't bother reiterating; he simply nodded, smiled, and patted the stone bench again until I lowered myself down onto it, still staring at his face as if it was the first human face I had ever come across. I was close enough to smell the clean scent of him, but not close enough for our legs to brush. He quickly remedied that by sliding an inch nearer and placing his hand on my knee, all the while studying me with two of the bluest, most inquisitive eyes I had ever seen.

When I could tear my own eyes away from them, I found myself gazing down at the hand covering my knee. The clean sinews on the back of his hand were covered with strawberry tinted hairs that shone in the morning sun like strands of woven gold. His forearm was well muscled and, like his hand, covered with a luscious stand of golden-red hair, just as golden-red as the hair atop his handsome head. That hair spilled over his forehead, and when he blinked his glorious blue eyes, the long blond lashes around them would nudge the hair aside to clear his vision. There was a tiny spray of freckles across his nose. My new young god had the sort of pale, delicate skin that would never darken noticeably in the sun but would forever remain as light as tea with milk cooling in a cup.

He saw where I was staring and flexed his fingers for my benefit before laying them back on my knee. "It's just a hand," he said, smiling.

Looking up, I was once again lost in the beauty of those heavenly blue eyes.

Somewhere in the eaves above our heads, a muted thumping of wings erupted in the shadows. An excited birdsong filled the air. We both lifted our heads to see what the commotion was all about. It was a flock of birds exploding from a hiding place in the eaves of the mission wall. The birds gathered together in midair and swooped off into the trees at the edge of the mission walls.

"Starlings?" I asked my companion.

He laughed. "Swallows," he said.

I blushed. This was springtime, and we were sitting in the mission garden at San Juan Capistrano. "Of course," I breathed. "What else would they be?"

He watched me turn red with a sort of awe that made me more excited than embarrassed. It was as if, at that very moment, he had eyes for no one else in all the world but me. Which I suppose he didn't, considering the fact we were the only two people in sight.

"What is your name?" he asked softly.

"David," I said. "David Ayres."

Again, the young god flexed his fingers atop my knee, causing a shudder to course through me. My shudder made his eyes open wide as he continued to study me sitting there beside him. The faintest trace of a smile turned up the corners of his mouth.

"I'm Arthur," he said. "Arthur Smith. I'm from Liverpool."

"Like the Beatles," I said.

He grinned, displaying snow white teeth, slightly crooked, and just the tip of a tongue as he licked the grin from his lips. "Yes. Like the Beatles."

Desperately seeking a way to continue the conversation without looking like an idiot, I said, "You don't sound like the Beatles. Your accent is—umm—classier."

He laughed. "You have a good ear. I was actually raised in Cornwall. Penzance, to be precise."

"Like the *Pirates of*," I beamed.

"Yes, sir. Like Gilbert and Sullivan's *Pirates of.*"

Having ran that conversational thread into the ground, we let silence settle over us, and as it did, his hand left my knee and he turned more completely toward me on the stone bench. His knee pressed into mine. When he had my full attention—which in reality he had commanded all along—he laid his hand against my cheek. I was so surprised by the touch, I gave a tiny gasp.

"Do you mind?" he asked in the merest whisper.

"N-no," I said, feeling the heat of his fingertips against my ear.

We sat like that for what seemed forever, his hand on my cheek, his eyes burrowing into mine. Time stood still around me. I heard the swallows return to the eaves above our heads. The bees droned among the tulips in the flower bed behind the bench, and the morning sun continued to peek across the mission wall to warm the air around us.

Finally, he broke the silence. "Are you here alone?"

"Yes. Are you?"

"Yes."

I heard a train whistle over by the tracks between us and the ocean. At the sound of it, he looked away from me at last. "I was going to take the early train down the coast to Del Mar. But if you're staying here, maybe I'll wait a day or so. Would you like to have lunch with me?"

"Yes. And dinner."

He laughed. "And maybe breakfast tomorrow?"

At the incredible prospect *that* question raised, I found no laughter inside me at all. I merely nodded my head, still lost in the depths of his azure eyes, which I now noticed perfectly matched the color of the California sky above our heads.

"I—"

"Yes?" he asked. "What were you about to say?"

I cleared my throat. "I was about to say I'm driving down the coast as soon as I finish piddling around here. I can drive you to Del Mar if you like."

"Tomorrow?" he asked.

I shrugged. "Tomorrow. The next day. A year from now. Whenever."

He laughed. "You are rather lackadaisical with your piddling."

I still couldn't find a laugh inside me. "I seem to be, don't I?"

Arthur took my hand with a gentle smile. "Walk with me," he said.

I RAPPED at Arthur's bedroom door and stepped inside without waiting for an invitation. The room smelled of Bengay and Lavoris.

Arthur was nowhere to be seen. I stepped through the sliding doors beside the bed and walked out onto the deck. The day was humid and in the high nineties. The sun hit me in the face like a hot towel. Arthur was lying back on a lounge chair with a book propped up on his chest. He wore a big fat pair of sunglasses over his regular bifocals. The sunglasses had been given to him at the time of his cataract surgery the year before. I had a pair just like them.

Getting old not only sucks, sometimes it simply isn't a lot of fun.

Sylvester lay sprawled out between Arthur's legs, pestering a catnip mouse.

Arthur looked up when I stood over him, casting him and Sylvester into shadow.

"Oh, good," he said, only half-joking. "Stay right there. The sun is blinding me."

"You'll die of a heat stroke out here. Come inside, and I'll make you some lunch."

"Is your jogger gone?"

"I don't know what you're talking about."

He barked a laugh. There wasn't much humor in it. "Bollocks. I'm sure you were standing at the front window with a stonker watching him clomp past."

His British colloquialisms made me smile, just as they always did. "You're American now, Arthur. No American ever said 'bollocks.' Ever. No American ever said 'stonker' either. We say 'bullshit' and 'hard-on,' as you damn well know. Would you like me to fix you some lunch?"

He carefully lifted the fat sunglasses from his head; the bifocals beneath were swept aside. When he closed the book, I noticed he was using the dandelion I had given him as a bookmark. He stared up at me with the same blue eyes I remembered from that day forty years earlier at the mission in San Juan Capistrano. The reddish-blond hair had lightened considerably since then, sprinkled as it was now with gray. The face around the eyes had withered and crinkled a bit with age. The eyes themselves were still glorious, even squinting against the sun as they were now.

I still enjoyed feeling them on me.

"I'm not hungry," he said.

"You need to eat."

"I'll eat later."

I remembered the smell of Bengay in the other room. "Bengay isn't going to help you. You have a pinched nerve. Or you pulled something. You need rest and maybe a cold pack."

"We'll see if the Bengay works first."

"God, you're stubborn."

He smiled. "Would you like to sit with me? We can have a chin wag."

"It's too hot out here."

He watched me standing there beside him. When he was finished watching, he gave out with a sigh. "There was a time when you would have sat on a fucking blowtorch to be near me and wouldn't have noticed the heat at all."

"Young love," I said.

He smiled a sad little smile. "Yes. Young love."

He turned away, and redonned both pair of glasses, one after the other. Settling into his chair, he once again opened the book he was holding and propped it on his chest. With his other hand, he idly scratched Sylvester under the ear.

I stared out at the canyon beside the house and watched a hawk swoop across the springtime sky. I remembered the flock of swallows that had witnessed two young humans sitting beneath them on a stone bench on a long-ago spring morning, and when that memory was firmly entrenched in my mind, I looked down at Arthur, now studiously ignoring me, then turned and walked back into the house.

SOMEHOW, OVER the years, the excitement in our relationship had dwindled to become simply—*comfort.* We did not argue. We did not fight. But worse than that, we rarely laughed. We simply lived. Under the same roof.

In a way retirement had not been kind to us.

Our interests had taken divergent turns. Arthur worked out at his health club a gazillion times a week, met every Tuesday in the park with his track club, ran marathons, biked to hell and gone on the weekends, and spent Saturday nights at Mass, where he had assumed the role of Eucharistic minister, assisting the priest in distributing Holy Communion to the congregation.

While Arthur filled his days with these interests, I filled my days with mine. I worked in the garden for hours on end. For exercise I walked, miles and miles. Occasionally Arthur would walk with me, but more often than not, I walked my miles alone. I also spent copious amounts of time writing letters and e-mails to old friends, people I had not seen for years and would probably never see again.

One day as I was writing at the computer, Arthur stepped into the den and laid a hand on my shoulder.

"Write to me," he said softly.

I swiveled in my chair and gazed up at him. "I don't need to write to you, love. You're right here."

Arthur chewed on his lip as he stared down at me. I saw him glance at the pages and pages I had written to a cousin in Indiana who I hadn't seen in thirty years. He blinked at the computer screen, then turned his eyes back to me.

"Write me a love letter," he said.

I laughed. "Aren't we a little old for love letters?"

He brushed his blond-gray hair away from his forehead, and to my amazement a blur of tears suddenly shone in his eyes.

"Maybe we are," he said and turned and walked away.

That had happened almost a year ago, and I had still not written Arthur a love letter.

For the life of me, I couldn't imagine why.

ARTHUR AND I shared an early lunch in a backyard café situated behind a gorgeous old Victorian house, which stood so close to the railroad tracks that when a train trundled past, the silverware rattled on the table. Across the tracks, the mission walls stood tall and sepia toned, giving mute contrast to the modern, colorful city that had built up around them, with its blaring car horns and glass office buildings.

The food in the backyard café was atrocious. I ordered a steak sandwich, and Arthur ordered clam chowder in a bowl of sourdough bread. His bread bowl had a tear in it, and all the while he ate, his chowder dribbled out across the tablecloth.

Arthur found that immensely amusing. "They'll have a devil of a time getting that stain out," he whispered with a twinkle in his heavenly blue eyes.

My steak sandwich was so tough I gave up on it after two bites, which I was still chewing ten minutes later. We laughed so hard the waitress merely stared at us, appalled.

"What do you do?" I asked, gnawing on a french fry that wasn't in much better shape than the steak. "I mean, what do you do for a living?"

"I don't know yet," Arthur said with a wicked grin. "Mum and Dad got tired of that answer and shipped me off to figure it out. So here I am. Touring the colonies."

"Hate to break it to you, but we're not colonies any longer. We have our own flag and everything."

"Oh, yes. That garish stripy-starry-flappy thing."

"Bingo."

"Where are you staying?" I asked, simply because I couldn't bear not to.

Arthur lowered his eyelids to half-mast and blessed me with a sexy, sinister smirk. "Ah, now we're getting to it, then."

He leaned toward me, elbows planted on the edge of the table, carefully avoiding the spilled chowder, and I sat mesmerized as his face softened and a gentle gust of wind stirred his hair. "I'm staying at a quaint little bed and breakfast less than a two-minute walk from this very spot. And by the way, you are the most stunning American I've seen on my trip. Did you know that?"

I could feel my blood—part of it anyway—rising to my face. The rest was sluicing downward through my veins and arteries to my crotch, where the fabric of my trousers seemed to be tightening all of a sudden. Sort of an impromptu shrinkage. Unless, of course, there was another reason for it.

"Uh, no," I said, a little breathless. "I *didn't* know that." I gave myself a couple of heartbeats to let my nerves settle down before asking, "Are you sure those gorgeous blue eyes of yours are working properly?" I held up my hand, a few fingers splayed. "How many fingers am I holding up?"

When I get rattled, I get sarcastic. It's a character flaw. So sue me.

Arthur smiled, still nailing me to my chair with those electric eyes. "You think my eyes are gorgeous, dear colonist?"

I nibbled on my lower lip and rolled my eyes across the heavens looking for divine help. Not seeing any, I decided to go with the truth. "I think all of you is gorgeous."

"That sentence can't be right, can it?"

"Seems right to me." *Truer words were never spoken.*

"No, I mean grammatically."

"Oh."

Again, Arthur's face softened. He reached out across the table with both hands and scooped my paw into a warm prison. My pulse hammered in my head at the feel of his skin against mine.

"Your hands are moist," he said.

"Nervous."

"I wonder if I explored you thoroughly, I might not find any other moist bits."

Not only did my pulse hammer in my head at that observation, but my heart lurched like it suddenly needed a little more room to work its magic.

No sense lying. For the first time ever, my dick was dripping during lunch. *That* sure as hell had never happened before. God bless the British.

"I think you probably would," I managed to squeak out. My normal baritone voice seemed to have been replaced by the squeal of a baby goat. "My armpits are certainly wet."

"I wasn't talking about your armpits."

"I know you weren't."

He pushed his strawberry blond hair away from his face and sat back in his chair, releasing my hand from his. It broke my heart a little bit to lose the connection.

"Would you like to see where I'm staying?" he asked.

"At this point in my life, that curiosity is tantamount in my mind."

"Wordy," he grinned. "I like that."

He reached into his pocket and dragged out a credit card. Waving a hand at the waitress—who was acting like she wasn't watching our every move but most certainly was—Arthur motioned for the check.

"Let me," I offered.

He shushed me with a beautiful lean finger pressed to his lips. "My parents are rich," he said. "Are your parents rich?"

"No."

"Then the nosh is on me."

"Okay." I wasn't happy about it. I was so smitten I wanted to do *something* for the man across from me.

He must have seen the disappointment on my face. He reached out again and patted the back of my hand. "You can buy breakfast," he said. "If we go to bed now—" He checked his wristwatch. "—at 11:53 in the forenoon, and then proceed to have sex eight or nine times, we should be good and hungry by tomorrow morning."

*Eight or nine times?*

All of a sudden my palms were sweaty, my ass was itching, and my dick was snaking down the leg of my pants. *How the hell was I going to walk down the street?* I swallowed with an audible gulp.

"I—I guess by then we'll be downright *starving*," I managed to squeak.


ARTHUR'S SECOND-STORY room at the bed and breakfast was small and sunny and very New Englandy for the West Coast, with lace curtains on the leaded windows and a floral print canopy over the bed. The view from said window wasn't exactly spectacular since the grand Pacific Ocean was nowhere in sight. Nope. Arthur's view looked out over another of the courtyard restaurants that seemed to be so popular in San Juan Capistrano. I could only assume the food in *that* courtyard restaurant would be an improvement over the food in the one *we* had lunched in.

I turned from the window and surveyed the room.

A spray of wildflowers stood in a crystal vase on a spindly round table by the door. The flowers' fragrance permeated the room. The bedspread on the wide four-poster bed was the same floral print as the canopy that hung above it. There were about a gazillion pillows scattered across the head of the bed, and the whole arrangement looked poufy and cutesy, and if I had to make that bed every morning, the first thing I would do would be throw all those damn pillows out the fucking window.

But I was too excited to contemplate the room's nelly-ass bed for very long. I was more intrigued by the room's human occupant, and frankly, there was nothing nelly about him at all.

Arthur closed the door behind us after ushering me inside, and as soon as the door was locked and he had given me time to ogle my surroundings, he walked directly into my arms.

"You're so beautiful," he said, gently grasping my waist and pulling me to him. When he laid his head on my shoulder and blew his warm breath across the side of my neck, I closed my eyes and buried my face in his hair. His golden locks smelled of cherry shampoo. With my hands at his back, our chests lay one against the other. I could feel every inch of his body against mine. We were both hard.

When he lifted his head from my shoulder and softly slid his lips over mine, I gave an ecstatic shudder. His eyes were wide open, never wavering from my face. I think he was gauging my reaction to his kiss. He didn't close his eyes until I began responding. I could feel his tongue seeking entrance, and eager to feel it against mine, I parted my lips to let it in. Only then did he close his eyes and give himself up completely to the kiss.

I quickly realized Arthur was a very good kisser. His soft lips did not simply lay atop my mouth, unmoving, disinterested, flaccid. He worked them. Exploring. Tasting. Prodding. His tongue, too, did not just stab into my mouth like an eel. He gently glided it over my own tongue, foraged across my teeth, making me feel things I had never felt with a kiss before. In the space of a dozen heartbeats, I was almost breathless with hunger for the man.

"Bed," I managed to mutter within the kiss, but rather than pull away at my plea to lead me toward the bed, he cupped the back of my head and kissed me all the harder where we stood.

His mouth was so silky and warm over mine, his breath so hot, the proddings of his seeking tongue so deliciously erotic, I had the distinct impression this was the first time I had ever been kissed by a man at all.

When he had me trembling in his arms, only then did he break the kiss and lead me by the hand to the edge of the bed.

He reached up to unbutton my shirt.

"It's so bright in here," I stammered.

John Inman

"Good," he breathed, his voice husky with desire. "I want to see every inch of you."

Something about his accent sent a renewed burst of desire shooting through me. He was so different from everyone I had ever known. So exotic. So alien. So sure of himself. So pale and smiling and sexy and strong.

"Oh God," I whispered. My knees were knocking. It wasn't stage fright. It was anticipation. Holy shit, I had never been this turned on in my life.

When his warm hand slid beneath the folds of my shirt and pressed itself to my breast, my desire instantly turned to an explosion of horror. *Oh, no. Oh dear God, no.*

*"Arthur, wait,"* I pleaded, but it was already too late, and I knew it.

I lunged forward, pressing my hips to his, and in a rush of shame and uncontrollable desire, I felt the come surge through my dick and soak my underwear. The orgasm was so powerful my knees buckled, and I buried my face in the crook of Arthur's neck while my seed shot out with the force of a Gatling gun. I bucked and gasped and ultimately squeezed my eyes shut in shame at what I had just done. As I emptied myself of seed, Arthur clutched me tight. My legs were trembling so violently his arms were the only things keeping me standing. Aside from the fact he was propping me up, I had no idea what Arthur's reaction was to what I had just done because I was too big a coward to open my eyes and look at his face.

He had to have figured it out, though, and the moment he spoke I realized he most certainly had.

"Oh, baby," he cooed, still keeping me wrapped in his arms as I tried to get myself under control. "That was the hottest thing I've ever experienced."

I could feel my shame afire on my face. My cheeks were burning. When I opened my eyes at last, I gazed sheepishly into Arthur's eyes, pleading for forgiveness. "I'm sorry, I—"

Before I could finish, his hand slid over my chest to caress my ribcage. Another shudder shot through me because my nerve endings were now so responsive to his touch I had to remind myself to breathe.

His voice was as shaky as mine. "Don't ever be sorry, David. Don't ever be. That was incredible."

Before I knew what was happening, he dropped to his knees in front of me and, with trembling hands, tore the clasp of my belt open, slid my zipper down out of the way, and pulled my pants to the floor. I looked down, still as ashamed as I had ever been in my life, and saw my white Jockey shorts, soaked with semen. Oddly enough, my cock was still hard.

With an incredulous smile on his face, Arthur slid his fingers beneath the waistband of my shorts, causing me to buck with desire yet again, and stripped them away before I could react. My come-soaked cock sprang up, and he immediately tucked it into his mouth. For balance more than anything else, I gripped the sides of his head as he drew my cock all the way in to the back of his throat. The semen splattered all over my pubic hair moistened his face, and when he felt it on his skin, he gazed up at me with those wondrously sexy eyes and grinned around my dick. I rose up on tiptoe as he drew his mouth slowly away from my cock, and the moment he was free of it, he spread his lips wide and sucked the come from my pubic hair. Every bit of it.

As he slavered over me, he tore at his own clothes, and when I saw what he was doing I began tearing at mine, kicking off my shoes and pants, stripping the unbuttoned shirt from my back. And the moment we were both naked, he once again took my cock into his mouth.

But it was my turn now, and I couldn't wait another second.

I gripped him under his armpits and pulled him to his feet. When his mouth slid over mine again, still damp with my come, I felt his steely cock press into me. He rose up on tiptoe as I had done and embraced me so hard he almost squeezed the air from my lungs.

"Bed," I gasped, and not waiting for him to say yes or no or maybe or what the fuck, I pulled him toward the four-poster and practically threw him onto it. He landed on his back and stared up at me, and when he gripped his cock as if to stroke himself, I slapped his hand away and crawled across the mattress to rest my head on his chest.

Arthur's pubic hair was strawberry blond, just like the hair on his legs. His chest was hairless, but the skin was so smooth and heated against my face as I dragged my lips downward across his belly that I couldn't bear to pull away from it. So even as I took his cock, which was uncut and heavily veined, into my hungry mouth and tasted him for the first time, I kept my hands splayed wide across his stomach just to feel the heavenly heat of it on my palms.

With his cock in my mouth at last, Arthur bucked beneath me and buried his hands in my hair, seeking to control my movements. Or so it seemed.

But apparently it was too late for him too.

As I finally relinquished my enjoyment of the taut flesh of his stomach to cup his balls in my hand instead, his hips gave one final spasmodic lunge upward, and with a cry he filled my mouth with his hot come. It surged out of him, jet after jet, like lava spilling from the lips of a volcano. When I couldn't keep up with the flow, he buried his cock deeper into my throat rather than let me go, and when his seed was spilling over my chin, I suddenly found myself laughing at the sheer perfection of it all.

He wrapped his strong, fuzzy legs around my head as he released the last drops of semen, and I cupped his ass to hold him in place against me as we both gradually relaxed into each other, our desires, for the moment, spent.

When I finally felt Arthur's softening cock slide from between my lips, I gazed up across the terrain of his luscious chest and saw him smiling down at me. His hands were still in my hair and he began softly stroking me there, his thumbs on my eyebrows, his fingertips on my ears.

I slid up in the bed just enough to lick a wayward drop of come from his stomach. I had no idea if the fluid was his or mine.

We lay there in that poufy-ass bed among those three hundred pillows for the longest time, not speaking, not surrendering the hold we had on each other.

Perhaps an hour later, when our cocks began to stir once more, we came together again. This time, we took our time about it.

Toward morning, when he entered me for the very first time and I felt his cock buried deep inside my ass, I twisted my head around to the side and sought his lips. Every inch of his body lay sprawled atop mine as his kiss and cock brought us completely together.

"You really are a David," he breathed over me. "You're beautiful."

When he came inside me, I almost wept.

# Chapter Two

SOMETIMES CHURCH services are so mind-numbingly boring you have to unleash your imagination just to survive, and boy, was my imagination in fine fettle today. For after all…

*…THE PRIEST was younger than my shoes. He stood at the urinal in a pair of sweat pants and a sweatshirt with a vee of sweat darkening the fabric from the back of his neck to his ass.*

*He was groaning and shaking the last drops of piss from his blessed dick.*

*I had just stepped from the toilet stall. Moving to the sink, I began lathering my hands. "Is something wrong, Father?"*

*He was still facing the urinal but he was no longer shaking the incense from his thurible, so to speak. He was simply holding himself upright and trying not to collapse like a house of cards.*

*"Cramp," he moaned, aiming a pair of deep brown eyes full of hurt in my direction with such force—and such passion—that he almost knocked me over. "Quads," he growled. "Killing me. I think I ran too far."*

*"What the hell is a quad?" I asked, trying not to lose myself in his eyes. Father Alessandro was from Guatemala. Twenty-six. A marathoner, like Arthur. It was Father Alessandro who brought me back into the church after an absence of, well, forever. It was not his God-marketing skills that brought me back. It was the fact that every time I watched him at the pulpit with his dark, handsome face and strong brown hands peeking through his vestments, I became instantly hard for the duration of services. Every Saturday evening. Every single one.*

Arthur thought I had returned to the church so I could see him perform his Eucharistic duties. I had not thought it wise to tell him what I was really doing there. Arthur is, after all, a wee bit jealous.

"Leg muscle," the good father said, throwing his head back and gritting his teeth, clinging to the urinal for all he was worth. It was then I noticed he had yet to tuck his cock back into his sweat pants. I suppose in the anguish of the moment, he had forgotten to do so.

"Is there anything I can do?" I asked, drying my hands with a wad of paper towels and carefully poking the used towels into the trash container provided. Father Alessandro had only last week bitched from the pulpit about the way parishioners were leaving the restrooms at the church a mess.

"A bit of massage would be a lifesaver," Father Alessandro said. "If you don't mind, I mean. Are you in a hurry to go somewhere, David? Can you spare a minute?"

"I would consider it my sacred duty," I said in all seriousness, never taking my eyes off the bobbing Guatemalan pecker, flaccid but lovely, hovering over the urinal. "Just turn this way, Father, and I'll see what I can do."

I lowered myself onto my knees before him as he swung his body around to face me. His face was still twisted in a rictus of misery. Mine, I'm sure, was twisted in a rictus of bliss.

"Just rub the front of my thigh," he said. "The left one. That's a good man."

With his luscious uncircumcised cock swinging sleepily in front of my face, I gripped his well-muscled thigh with both hands and began kneading it like a lump of bread dough.

Again the good father threw his head back and emitted a groan. This groan sounded considerably happier than the others that had preceded it.

"Higher," he muttered. "Harder."

So I moved my hands higher and added a little more enthusiasm to the endeavor. With my hands situated where they now were, at every ministration I bumped his ball sac with the back of my fingers and, not unlike watching a *blossom unfold in slow motion, I stared, mesmerized, as his brown cock twitched and lengthened and, in a final surge of power, stood upright like that iconic flagpole rising over the rocks on Iwo Jima. The good father's shiny cockhead peered through the folds of his foreskin, and it was all I could do not to lick my lips staring at it. Father Alessandro's legs began to shake. I guess my massage was doing wonders for his quads. It certainly seemed to have done wonders for his dick. Not to mention my own.*

*I was seriously considering making a large financial contribution to the church when Father Alessandro looked down upon me and laid his lovely strong hand atop my head in blessing. He took a teeny step forward on his apparently much-improved leg and pressed the underside of his cock against my face.*

*The satiny heat of that beautiful cock snuggled alongside my nose made me suck in a great gout of grateful air, and as I sucked in the air, I sucked in the cock as well.*

*Father Alessandro rose up on tiptoe, proving to me once and for all that his quads were now in tip-top shape, and stabbed his dick all the way to the back of my throat. As he pumped his delicious pecker in and out of my mouth, causing us both to tremble in delight, he seemed to feel the urge to make conversation.*

*"In my country," he said, "we prize older men for their wisdom."*

*I nodded and mumbled something around his dick that sounded a little like "Good to know."*

*He smiled down at me with beatific patience. "You don't have to answer," he said, once again pushing his dripping cock toward my gullet before easing it out again. "I can see you're busy."*

*I nodded, which was about the extent of my capabilities at the moment. Or so I thought.*

*Father Alessandro cupped my cheeks in his hand and slid his cock free of my lips. He swayed his hips to rub his hardness back and forth across my face, smearing a trail of spit and precome across the bridge of my nose from one ear to the other. Gently he said, "Rise up, David. I have the urge to take this one step further if you've no objection."*

*"None whatsoever," I managed to mumble, so turned on I was beginning to wonder if my pacemaker was about to short circuit. "I'm at your complete disposal, Father. Anything I can do for the church. You know that."*

*"Then stand and face the sink for me, sir," Father Alessandro urged, and I did as he asked. The minute my hands were on the sink and my face was crammed up against the mirror, I felt the father's strong fingers reaching around to undo my belt buckle, zip down my trousers, and pull my pants all the way down until they were bunched around my ankles.*

*In the mirror I saw the father turn and flip the lock on the bathroom door. When he saw me watching him, he smiled sweetly and said, "So we won't be interrupted. You don't wish to be interrupted, do you, David?"*

*Dumb question. With his hands now on my ass, spreading my cheeks apart, I decided the question must be rhetorical, so I didn't bother to answer. The good father didn't seem to notice.*

*"You are in remarkable shape for a man your age," the father said. "I'm truly impressed. Your posterior is lovely. Many don't survive the ravages of time, I understand. Just exactly how old are you, David?"*

*"I'm sixty-four," I said with a tremble as the father's thumb did a gentle slide across my opening. "Arthur just turned sixty," I needlessly added.*

*"Remarkable," he said again.*

*He reached around me to pump a couple of squirts of hand soap into his hand from the dispenser on the wall, and just as my heart was beginning to hammer like a big fat woodpecker, he spread the hand soap along the cleft of my ass. Without waiting around to ask directions or do a Google search, he buried a finger all the way up my bunghole. I wiggled my ass backward to get the last knuckle in there, and Father Alessandro whispered, "Bless you, my son."*

John Inman

*I centered my eyes on his handsome brown face in the mirror as he pushed his sweat pants down past his hips and laid his erect cock into the crack of my ass like a hot dog in a bun. His dick was still moist from my spit and several smears of precome, and without further ado, he simply pressed the fat wet head of it to my opening and burrowed his way in. He slid into me without a single hitch, and by the time his forest of Guatemalan pubic hair was scraping the tender skin around my welcoming asshole, I had upped the check on my donation by adding another zero to the total.*

*He pumped his stiff cock into my opening until I could hardly catch my breath. My own cock was rubbing the cool porcelain on the edge of the sink, and after one particularly vigorous stroke inward of the good father's cock during which he scraped my prostate so deliciously I thought I would faint, I came instead. My jism squirted into the sink as I reached around behind me to pull Father Alessandro deeper into my ass.*

*"Oh my goodness," he muttered with his lips to my ear, leaning over me and grinding my still dripping dick into the sink. The moment the words were out of his mouth, he gave a lurch, gripped my stomach with both hands to hold me close, and shot his hot come into my bowels, squirt after lovely squirt.*

*We both stood there convulsing, me with my dick in the sink, him with his dick in me. We shook like a couple of aspen trees as we emptied ourselves out.*

*When his cock began to soften inside me, he whispered into my ear, "I believe my leg is better now, David. Thank you so much for your assistance."*

*"Don't you mean thank you so much for my ass?"*

*He giggled sweetly and poked a tongue in my ear—just to be kind, I'm sure. I was, after all, considerably older than he. "I suppose thanking you for your ass would be more appropriate. Still, it seems to have done the trick. My leg feels great."*

*"I'm so glad." And I was too.*

*As he pulled his dick slowly free of me, inch by heavenly inch, I felt one last dribble of come erupt from my own, causing me to shudder in a last-ditch spout of ecstasy.*

34

*"Tell Arthur I said hello, won't you, David? We're so happy to have him participate at Saturday services. He is fulfilling his duties splendidly. Tell him I said so, won't you?"*

*"You bet, Father," I said, wondering why he hadn't praised my services, which in my opinion were considerably more personal than Arthur's.*

*He gave my face a kindly pat as I pulled up my trousers. "Good man," he said, tugging his sweat pants up over his ass and tucking in his dick. "Good man."*

*I'm not entirely sure, but I think I blushed.*

ARTHUR AND I shook hands with Father Alessandro as we exited the church. The good father's handsome, smiling face was all over us. While the Catholic Church might not be 100 percent on board the gay train, Father Alessandro, at any rate, didn't seem to have a problem with it at all.

"I'm glad you both could make it this evening, gentlemen." He looked out across the darkening California sky. The sun was down and evening shadows were just beginning to cool the pavement. "It's going to be a beautiful night."

"Thank you, Father," Arthur said, returning the smile with one of his own high-beam stunners. "And you have a nice Sunday too."

Father Alessandro shrugged. "Just another workday," he grinned. "Save a soul, sprinkle a baby." We all laughed.

Arthur and I strolled down the front steps and headed for the car.

"I'll tell him tomorrow," Arthur said, lowering his voice so the other parishioners walking along beside us couldn't overhear.

"Tell who what?"

"Father Alessandro. I'm going to tell him I quit."

"You mean the church?"

"Blimey, no. Just the Eucharistic minister gig."

I couldn't believe what Arthur was telling me.

"But *why* are you quitting? I thought you loved it."

Arthur stopped in the middle of the sidewalk and reached down to pull off his shoes and socks.

My mouth flopped open in surprise. "What the hell are you doing?"

Arthur blinked and regarded his bare feet as if they were the oddest things he had ever seen in his life. "I'm not sure." Then he smiled, ignoring the surprised looks of the people passing us by. "Oh, I remember now. My toes were hot."

"That's ridiculous."

"Thank you." And we recommenced our stroll toward the car, me full-blown confused by the way Arthur was acting, and Arthur whistling a merry tune while dangling one shoe and one sock each from either hand as he ambled along.

I gave up on the shoes. "Fine. Your toes are hot. But what about the church thing?"

"What church thing?"

I huffed out an annoyed little puff of air. I grabbed him by the elbow and dragged him to a stop. When I had his full attention, I stuck my fists on my hips and glared at him like an irate schoolmarm down to her last ounce of patience. "You know damned well what church thing. Why are you giving up your gig as St. Patrick's Eucharistic minister, Arthur? You love Saturday service. You love rehearsing your scriptural readings in front of the bedroom mirror. Since you don't work anymore, going to church is the only occasion you have to get dressed up. You love that too."

"I wore my fancies for your cousin's wedding."

"That was twenty years ago!"

He considered that. "Really? It seems like yesterday."

I huffed again. "And *church*?"

Arthur offered up one of his sweet smiles, the kind that used to have me out of my trousers in ten seconds flat. "Oh, I'm not going there anymore."

"So you mean you *are* quitting the church completely?"

"Yes. Didn't I tell you?"

And with that, he turned and padded off toward the parking lot, tugging me along behind him like a pull toy. "Hurry along, David. We're going to miss Lawrence Welk."

So for lack of a better plan, I hurried along. What the hell else was I supposed to do?

ARTHUR'S STRONG young arms circled me as we lay there in our nest of throw pillows, listening to the swallows chattering up a storm outside the window. The sun was up, barely, and through the B&B's lace curtains, the light cast tiny patterned shadows over our naked skin.

I snuggled my cheek to Arthur's chest while he pressed his lips into my hair. I could hear the soft thunder of his heartbeats, feel the rise and fall of his gentle breathing.

I plucked one of his hands from my shoulder and stared at it, flexing the fingers wide, stroking the skin at his wrist. When he playfully tweaked my nose between his thumb and forefinger, I pressed my mouth to his palm and inhaled his scent for the thousandth time. I couldn't seem to get enough of it.

"What are you going to do in Del Mar?" I asked.

He shrugged. "Nothing much. I saw in the dailies they are holding a fair there at the fairgrounds. Thought I'd give it a peek."

"Can I go with you?"

He giggled as he pressed his lips more firmly into my scalp. "Silly question."

I lifted my head to gaze into those eyes one more time. The eyes I simply could not get enough of. "Why is it silly?"

He pulled his hand from my mouth and cupped the back of my head, incinerating me with his stare. There was a soft smile on his lips. It was the same smile I had seen there the last time he was in the throes of orgasm. Sexy as all get out. "It's silly because you never have to ask if you can go with me. Anywhere."

"No?"

"No. Just assume that I want you there beside me. Okay?"

John Inman

"Okay."

"Don't even ask."

"Okay. I won't ask."

I returned his smile and pushed my face into his chest again. I couldn't seem to make my smile go away. It just wouldn't leave. Earlier I had tucked my hand between Arthur's legs, just to be cozy, and now his balls were lying snug atop my fingertips. He squeezed his legs together, trapping my hand further in the heavenly heat of his crotch—the crotch I now knew as well as I knew my own.

Breathing in the scent of him and once again feeling the pulsing of his heart against my face, I muttered, "Thank you."

And once more his strong young arms wrapped themselves around me, pulling me close. He buried his luscious lips in my hair again. Remarkably, I could feel my dick begin hardening against his hip. My hunger for man flesh should have been slaked four orgasms ago—or was it five? I couldn't remember.

When Arthur eased me onto my back and slid downward in the bed to draw my cock into his mouth yet again, I closed my eyes and let him take me where he would. Then he freed my dick from his mouth and laid it over his lips, inhaling the heat of it as he gazed across my stomach to my face.

As always, he was smiling. "The folks thought a tour of America with all the butch Yanks would straighten me out."

He nudged my dick, which left a smear of precome across his cheek.

"How's that working out for you, then?" I asked. "Noticeably straighter yet?"

"Not that I've noticed."

He wiggled around in the bed until he was stretched out beside me in the opposite direction. Once he was comfortable, he pressed his cock to my lips, just as I was doing to his. I smiled and made it mine once more.

When he came, it was the sweetest come I had ever tasted. I knew the taste of Arthur now. I knew it as well as I

38

knew the taste of sugar. In fact, I craved that sweetness every moment I was with him.

Then it was my turn to come. I arched my back into him as he cupped my ass in his hands, holding me tight. He laughed and gurgled as my come filled his mouth.

When I was empty, he continued to suck me until I had nothing left to give. Only then did we doze.

Still holding on for dear life.


WE ATTENDED morning mass at the Serra Chapel, located inside the east gate of the old mission. Raised in a totally unreligious family, Catholic Mass was a new experience for me. Taking pity on me, what with me being out of my element and all, Arthur steered us into the rearmost pew in the beautiful old chapel. We sat close enough that our legs touched. If Arthur found that inappropriate for a church service, he certainly didn't let on. In fact, all through Mass he rested his hand on my knee. The first time we had to stand in prayer, I did so with an embarrassing erection.

"I thought most Brits weren't Catholic," I whispered, standing next to Arthur, my hands folded over my crotch to hide the bulge. "I thought you guys were all Anglican."

He grinned, his downward glance telling me he knew full well why my hands were positioned where they were. "A few of us are Catholic." He nudged me with an elbow. "Whip out your biggie. I want to see it."

"Shut up!" I hissed, feeling the blood creep up the back of my neck and flood my cheeks. An old woman in the pew in front of us turned and scowled in our direction. Arthur waggled his fingers at her in greeting. She grunted and said, "Harrumph" before turning back around.

It was apparently all too much for Arthur. The old woman, the biggie (as he called it), my embarrassment. He took my hand and tugged me along the length of the pew, trying not to smash the toes of any other worshippers along the way, and when he had me in the aisle, we all but ran through the chapel doors and across the mission plaza to get back out onto the street. By the time we were there, Arthur was doubled over in laughter.

"Well, that was uncomfortable," he sputtered, tears streaming down his cheeks.

I was so relieved to be out of the church, I didn't even mind that he was laughing at me. In fact, I had other things on my mind. One, I was hungry. And two, I still had a boner.

Before I knew what I was going to say, it was already said. "When are you going back to England?"

He wiped happy tears from his cheeks, his grin still splitting his face from ear to ear. "Why? Are you sick of me already?"

"No," I said. "I don't want you to go at all. I want you to stay here. With me."

His laughter bubbled to silence. He blinked back the remaining tears in his eyes and simply stood there, clutching his chest, leaning on a parking meter and staring at me.

His stare was delicious. Which didn't alleviate my boner even one little bit.


THE SURF bubbled deliciously over my bare toes. The water was cold, the sand hot. I rolled my pant legs up to my knees because I hadn't packed shorts or a bathing suit.

Arthur wore Bermuda shorts that were the ugliest things I had ever seen. The lean pale legs poking out the bottom of them were the most *beautiful* things I had ever seen. Arthur's golden leg hair shimmered in the rays of the setting sun dancing across the waves. The sunset seemed to have stirred up the first breeze I had felt since this long hot day of sightseeing and sex began.

It was without a doubt the best vacation I had ever spent, and it was only our third day together in the little beach town of San Juan Capistrano. We had been trying to decide where to go next. North to Disneyland. South to the fair in Del Mar. East to the desert. I didn't care what our destination was. I simply wanted to be with Arthur. For me it didn't get any more complicated than that. I wasn't sure what he wanted, although he didn't seem averse to having me tag along beside him. I must say, though, if a propensity for making love was any indication, he was just as smitten as I was. At least I hoped he was.

"You have a lovely country," Arthur said beside me. My hand was corralled in his, and we were strolling through the breakers, splashing and giggling and enjoying the feel of the water. There were no other humans in sight, although we could tell by the occasional train rumbling along the tracks beside the beach, or the jarring blast of a car horn now and then on the highway that traversed the California coastline that the world was still plodding along around us. While people might be nowhere in sight from our vantage point, the swallows were still there—swooping across the sand or circling high above our heads with their sharp little cries splitting the air. As they had done the past two evenings, we knew they would disappear at sunset, folding themselves into their nests in the eaves of the old mission, resting from their exertions, guarding their newly laid eggs, waiting for the day they would return to wherever they spent the other half of their lives. A far-off jungle perhaps, or another city a continent away from this one.

Arthur seemed to divine what I was thinking. "I love the swallows," he said, dragging me to a stop so we could sit in the sand and stare out at the orange sun dipping behind the water. "I love the way they dance in the air. The way they sing every minute of the day. The way they are always happy."

His hand still caressed mine. Our shoulders brushed. We sat cross-legged in the sand, and his bare knee pressed hard against my exposed calf. Occasionally I closed my eyes to better concentrate on the rasp of his leg hair scraping over mine. Just that simple touch made me long to hold him naked in my arms yet again.

Arthur was a drug. And I was already addicted. I knew it beyond all doubt. My only question was whether he knew it too.

"What is your home like in San Diego?" he asked, turning to study my face. "Do you have family there?"

"No," I said. "My parents died when I was young. I was raised by an aunt in Indiana. I came here right out of high school and never looked back."

"You weren't happy there? It's rural, isn't it? Indiana?"

"Yes. And puritanical. I could never have been what I am living there."

He smiled softly. "And what are you?"

"Gay."

He nodded then, as if he suddenly understood. "Ah."

I didn't want to talk about myself. I wanted to talk about Arthur. I wanted to talk about Arthur *and me*.

I could hear my pulse thudding in my head as I forced myself to ask the question. I wasn't sure I wanted to hear the answer, but I knew I couldn't go any longer without knowing one way or the other. "When do you have to go home, Arthur? How long can you stay in the States?"

"I began my trip with a ninety-day visa. Twenty days are already gone."

"So you have a little over two months left."

"Yes."

"How do you go about staying longer?"

"I'm not sure. Why, David? Do you think I should?"

"Yes, Arthur. I think you should."

"Why?"

I looked down at the sand between my legs. The surf had risen enough to almost reach us with every fourth or fifth incoming little wave. Soon we'd have to move, or our asses would get soaked. Like I cared.

"I don't want to scare you away," I said.

He aimed his eyes at me and twisted his torso around to really stab me with his stare. "What makes you think you

42

would scare me away? Are you going to do something scary to me?" There was no smile in his words. He was serious.

"Maybe," I said. The word came out as a whisper. I hadn't meant it to; it just did.

Finally, a smile peeked through on Arthur's face. It came from his eyes. A gust of wind lifted the hair from his forehead, and I reached up to feel the softness of that great mop of gold stirring in the breeze. His hair was hot from the sun, the golden-reddish threads of it as fine as silk between my fingers. Arthur lifted his hand to stroke the underside of my arm, sending a chill through me. It was that simple touch that gave me the strength to say what I wanted to say.

"I have to go back to work Monday. That's two days away. When I go back to the city, I want you to come with me. I'll show you San Diego. You can stay at my apartment. It's tiny, but we'll make do. You won't have to pay for a hotel. You'll save some money."

His eyes narrowed as his fingers continued to stroke my arm. We both edged our butts a little farther up the beach when a wee wave gently nudged us where we sat. "It's a dangerous enterprise you're offering, David."

"I—I don't understand what you mean, Arthur."

"I think you do. I think you can see the danger in my eyes. Just as I can see the danger in yours."

"I want to be with you," I said, fighting back my fear at what I was saying. I felt my eyes burn as if tears were on the way. My heartbeat once again began pounding in my head. I was afraid. I was terrified. I couldn't stop myself from saying the words. "I don't want you to leave me yet. I haven't had enough of you, Arthur. I don't think I'll *ever* have enough of you."

His eyes finally left my face. His fingertips receded from my forearm. He stared out at the sunset on the ocean, closed his eyes for a moment as the cooling breeze brushed his face. We were still pressed together, and he laid his hand on my leg and gently brushed the hair on my shin. I gave a shudder at his touch.

When he spoke, there was sadness in his voice. I had never heard sadness there before. It broke my heart to hear it.

"David, if you feel that way now, how do you think you'll feel if we spend the next two months together? Don't you think it will make my going back to England even harder?"

"I don't care," I said.

And he turned his eyes to me once again. "But what about me, David? Don't you think it will make it harder for me?"

I blinked. There was a lump in my throat as big as a cantaloupe. I tried to swallow it just to get the damn thing out of the way. "Does that mean—"

"Yes," he said. "That's exactly what it means."

"You like me?"

A tiny smile twisted the corners of his mouth. "If you want to call it that."

"Then will you stay with me in San Diego?"

"Yes. If that's what you want."

"I want it more than my next breath of air," I said softly.

When he laid his lips over mine—with the wind in our hair, our asses wet from the surf, and the roar of the ocean in our ears—I lost all concept of time. I was in another universe.

As the sun dipped completely below the horizon and the first new stars blinked into existence over our heads, I knew it was a universe I never wanted to leave.

The taste of his kiss convinced me.


FRESH OUT of the shower, I stood naked, staring at myself in the bathroom mirror. I was not a happy camper. While I had never been *particularly* pleased with my appearance, even when I was young, I was most *assuredly* not pleased with it now that I was well into my sixty-fourth year.

I still stood straight, kept my weight at what it was when I was in my thirties, and because of the miles of walking I did every day, my legs were still strong and well-muscled. They were still coated with dark hair, too, which Arthur still to this day loved above all my other attributes except my dick, or so he continually told me. My dick, by the way, was still in fine working order as well. Too fine, maybe, since it still pretty much controlled my every thought, just as it had when I was young.

It was the melted-candle look of my face that bothered me more than anything. My jowls drooped, or so I imagined. My ears had grown larger. (Surely that couldn't be true, could it?) And my eyelids appeared to hang above my eyes like sun visors. Yuck.

Of course, I knew I shouldn't complain. My health was good. All body parts were fully functional. I only needed glasses for reading. My teeth were my own. I wasn't bald.

Still, it saddened me to see no flame of youth staring back at me from that foggy bathroom mirror. No clean line of jaw. No smooth stretch of skin at the side of the eyes.

In truth, Arthur had aged far better than I. Perhaps it was his pale English skin, nurtured in his youth with the moist air of England. While I had deep lines at the sides of my mouth and bisecting my forehead, Arthur's face was still soft and relatively wrinkle free.

His blue eyes were still piercing and beautiful too.

And suddenly there they were, peering over my shoulder. Those incredible azure eyes. He grinned when I jumped in surprise to find him there.

"Boo." He laughed.

I grabbed a towel from the rod and quickly wrapped it around my waist. He laughed at that as well, although even with his laughter there was a hint of disappointment in his eyes.

"We've been together almost forty years, David. It's a little late for shyness now."

I clucked my tongue, just as old people are wont to do. I wasn't happy about the clucking, but it was a little late to do anything about it now.

"If I looked the way I did forty years ago, I wouldn't mind you barging in."

The hurt in his eyes deepened. "Is that what I did? Barged in?"

"You know what I mean, Arthur. It's—well, it's *embarrassing*. I don't want you looking at my saggy old ass."

His face creased into a weary smile. His eyes offered up a determined sparkle, and I could literally see him trying to push the hurt away. He pressed his lips to my shoulder and began sliding his tongue down my back. I didn't need a GPS to see where he was headed. "Your ass is anything but saggy," he muttered into my skin. And just as his tongue slid over the small of my back, he snaked a hand around to the front and dragged the damp towel away from my body, flinging it aside.

I tried to pull away. "It's too light in here. Jesus, Arthur! I'm trying to get cleaned up."

His tongue had found the cleft of my ass, and he was just beginning a gentle reconnaissance, which sent a shiver up my spine. It was a good shiver, but I still ignored it.

"Please, baby," he crooned, his hand now reaching around to cup my balls. "Just come for me. That's all I ask."

I stepped away and grabbed the towel he had tossed aside, wrapping it once again around my waist as I none too gently pushed him aside.

"Tonight," I said. "We'll have a date night. I promise."

Still on his knees, he looked up at me with a soulful look. I could see he was embarrassed. Embarrassed and hurt.

"All right," he said softly, grabbing the edge of the sink and pulling himself to his feet. "I'm sorry I bothered you."

He turned to go.

I caught his sleeve as he stepped away. "I'm just embarrassed," I said. "Surely you understand that."

He reached out and slid a hand along the length of my arm, caressing the hair there, stroking the skin still soft from my bath. As it had been for all the years I had known him, his

46

touch was gentle. Even his innate kindness was still there. Only the hurt was new.

"I'm sorry, David," he said, shaking his head, "but I don't understand at all."

With those words, he turned and walked away, silently closing the bathroom door behind him.

When I heard his footsteps receding down the hall, I once again faced myself in the mirror.

"Why?" I asked my reflection. "Why did you do that?"

I couldn't think of an answer.


IN MY youth I lived in a tiny one-bedroom garret apartment perched atop a lovely old Craftsman home in the Hillcrest section of San Diego. My landlord, Mr. B, was a gay octogenarian with a gay octogenarian lover known as Mr. C. The two men were sweet, rather feeble, and gentle with their rent. They had been together since roughly the time Moses led the children of Israel out of Egypt. Mr. B and Mr. C welcomed Arthur with open arms when I introduced them.

"Stay as long as you like," Mr. B said, tossing a wink first to Arthur, then to me, then to his partner. "Who am I to stand in the way of true love?"

"Who are *we*, you mean," Mr. C interrupted.

"Yes," Mr. B corrected himself. "Who are *we*?"

When Arthur and I both turned a lovely shade of pink and shuffled our feet a bit on their doorstep, Mr. C elbowed Mr. B in the ribs. "Look what you've done. You've gone and embarrassed them."

Mr. B backtracked like a politician caught with his mouth too far open. "Oh, dear, I'm afraid I have. Sorry, boys. Maybe that L-word hasn't been spoken yet." With another wink to everyone present, he added, "But never fear. If I am any judge, and I am, the word should be popping up shortly."

"If *we* are any judge," Mr. C interjected, causing Mr. B to roll his eyes heavenward.

"Yes," he said, just short of a growl. "If *we* are any judge."

"You're more than welcome here, Arthur," Mr. B said kindly, still pumping Arthur's arm like a jack handle. And in perfect unison, the two older men added, "Stay as long as you like." With a final wink, at me this time, Mr. B finally released poor Arthur, gently closed the door, and the two men went back to whatever activities gay octogenarian landlord lovers partake of in their free time.

As I led Arthur around the back of the house to the stairs leading up to my apartment, he took my hand as he always did when we were alone.

"Why would he think we're in love?" Arthur asked.

I shrugged, but it wasn't a very concerted one. "I don't know."

"Blimey, David. Are we that obvious?"

We were only three steps up the staircase when I yanked him to a stop. "What are you saying, Arthur?"

"I'm saying the old coot is pretty smart."

"Which one?"

"Both of them."

"B-because of what he said about the L-word and the fact that it should be popping into our lexicon pretty soon? Is that why they're smart?"

"Lexicon. Good word, David. And yes. Well, more prescient than smart."

"Prescient is a good word too," I said.

"Thank you. And yes, because of what he said about the L-word, ducks. How long have we known each other, do you think?"

"Three days and sixteen hours." I glanced at my watch. "No, wait. Almost seventeen hours."

Arthur blinked. "You have it down to the minute?"

"Well—"

He chucked me gently under the chin. After the chucking, his fingers lingered over my Adam's apple. They lingered there

48

just long enough to make me horny. Which took about three seconds.

"Maybe they're senile," I said, trying to ignore the tightening of my trousers in the general vicinity of my crotch. "Maybe old people see love everywhere they look."

Arthur's smile beamed brightly. "What a grand notion. Then I want to be old too."

For lack of an intelligent response to that, I instead glanced at my watch and said, "*Now* it's three days and seventeen hours. And six seconds," I added lamely.

Arthur's fingers were still caressing my throat. He gazed out over Mr. B's and Mr. C's rose garden at the back of the house.

"It's beautiful here," Arthur said, seemingly to himself. Then turning to me, he said, "David, what are we going to do when my ninety-day visa has expired?"

"Well, you'll have to get another one."

"I don't think it works that way."

"Then we'll figure something out, Arthur."

"Figure something out to what end, David?"

"To the end of you never leaving."

"That's a terrible sentence."

"Nice sentiment, though, don't you think?"

Arthur's eyes softened. Even his touch on my throat softened. "It is a lovely sentiment indeed, David. Would you fall over dead if I told you I loved you?"

My heart quickened. "I-I'm not sure."

"Then I'd better not risk it." Arthur smiled benignly.

"No, you'd better not."

"But if we're afraid to say it, then it's probably true. Right?"

"Right as rain," I said. I reached up to caress his face, one hand on either cheek. He immediately turned his head to kiss first one of my palms, then the other.

"Which puts us *really* in a pickle, Arthur."

"Love your Americanisms."

"Thank you."

"Love a few other things too. I even love saying I love a few other things."

"Not as much as I love hearing it."

Arthur grinned. "We're becoming maudlin."

"Yes, well, that's love for you. I mean, if that's what we're talking about." I watched as he glanced off again to the roses by the fence. I waited until his eyes were once again focused on me.

"I want you in my bed. Now." My throat was so tight I could barely get the words out.

He laid a hand flat against my chest. "Is there any hope at all that you also want me *here*? In your heart?"

"Arthur, you took up residence there with the first glimpse I had of you sitting on that stone bench in the mission garden."

"I don't believe in love at first sight."

"Neither do I."

"Perhaps it was hormones."

"Probably. And they're still kicking up a storm."

Arthur smiled. "I like the sound of that."

I took a deep breath, and at that precise moment, my eyes finally filled with tears. "It's too soon, Arthur. I don't think we should be talking about this quite yet. I don't trust myself not to say the word. You know. The word that starts with *L*. I just don't want to say it for a while."

His thumb slid a tender trail across my lips. "Then we won't. But will you promise me that one day, one day a lifetime away, we'll be like Mr. B and Mr. C? Will you promise me that?"

"Yes, Arthur. I promise you that. I promise you everything I have. I promise you everything I am and everything I will ever be. And someday I even promise the words."

Arthur cupped my chin in his fingertips and pulled me close. He took one step up the staircase so as to loom over me, and I tipped my head up to better lose myself in his eyes. Just before laying his lips to mine, he softly whispered, "That's all I ask. Just you and the words. Someday. The words."

As we stood in each other's arms and kissed on the old wooden steps leading up to my tiny apartment, which Arthur had not yet seen, we heard a pair of bedraggled old chuckles coming from the kitchen window beside the stairs.

"We're being watched." Arthur smiled into our kiss.

"Good." I smiled back, too lost in the taste of Arthur's lips to mind being eavesdropped upon.

I realized at that moment that sometimes words don't really need to be said at all. After all, they are always there on the air anyway. Hovering.

Like swallows.

# Chapter Three

THE TWO young men were perhaps eighteen and nineteen. One was black, the other Hispanic. They were decked out almost identically in white short-sleeve shirts, dark slacks, and black well-shined shoes. The young Hispanic was wearing white socks with his black pants, which I somehow found charming.

When I answered the door, I discovered them there, shoulder to shoulder, with Bibles in their hands, staring at me with hopeful, eager expressions on their young, guileless faces. Tall and lean, clear-eyed and well-groomed, they were an incredible gift to find on one's doorstep on this otherwise sweltering, molten Tuesday afternoon. And of course, my imagination took off like a shot…

*…THE BOYS, for that is how I thought of them although they were most certainly men, not boys, were sparkling with sweat. After traipsing from door to door for God knows how many hours peddling religion on this hot California day, anyone would have been sparkling with sweat.*

*Yes, that's what they were peddling all right. For they were Jehovah's Witnesses. And two of the loveliest Jehovah's Witnesses I had ever seen.*

*The first words out of the young black man's mouth were "Good morning, sir. Do you have God in your heart?"*

*The first words out of the young Hispanic's mouth were "If you do or if you don't, I wonder if we could have a few words with you on the subject?"*

*"Boys," I said, beaming like a lighthouse, "step inside out of the sun, and we'll chat to your heart's content. Perhaps you*

*would like some iced tea to cool yourselves down. It's hotter than a steel mill out here."*

*They looked at each other then back at me. It was fairly obvious by their reaction to my invitation they were more accustomed to people telling them to fuck off rather than asking them in for tea. I was happy that I could thus restore their faith in humanity. For after all, if a Jehovah's Witness can't find faith, then who the hell can?*

*"Come along," I said. "Don't be shy. While we're standing here, my air conditioning is being sucked through the door. Can't have that now. Otherwise there won't be any left for you. Air conditioning, I mean, not sucking," I corrected myself with a giggle.*

*My use of the word "sucking" seemed to have opened their eyes a bit, but I fear it was really the air conditioning that grabbed their attention. I stepped back from the door and ushered them inside like the liveryman waving the Queen Mother into the coach. They crossed my threshold with polite nods of their heads, one after the other, all smiles and with no small amount of gratitude beautifying their faces. Lordy, they were handsome.*

*I waved them onto the sofa by the front window. As soon as they were situated, I dragged the blinds closed on the large picture window behind them to block out the sun and cool them even more. As they settled back onto the cool leather of the couch, Bibles in their laps, they emitted a pair of delicious groans of ecstasy. Each young man then pulled a handkerchief from his back pocket and wiped the sweat from his face before stuffing the hanky back where it came from.*

*"Thank you," they said in unison. "We've been walking for hours," the young black man explained. "You're the first person all day to offer us refreshments."*

*I made a great show of slapping my forehead. "Refreshments! Of course! Let me get your tea while you two settle in and relax. Kick your shoes off if it'll make you more comfortable. You've been walking on the hot pavement for Lord knows how long. Your feet must be burning up as well."*

*With that, I shuffled off to the kitchen, where it so happened I had a large, fresh jug of sun tea cooling on the counter. I took two of my biggest tumblers from the cabinet, tossed in a few ice cubes, and filled them to the brim with tea. Then I added a sprig of mint. Just to be snooty.*

*I scurried back to the living room, placed a tumbler of iced tea in each of their hands, and parked myself on the edge of the coffee table directly in front of them. I sat so close that each of my knees touched one of theirs. I noticed they had indeed removed their shoes while I was gone. In fact, they had also removed their socks. I was more than happy to see they were not standing on principles. When it comes to comfort, we should all do everything we can to keep our bodies happy.*

*Giving them both a friendly pat on the knee, which made them blink in surprise, I bubbled, "Drink up, boys. And once you've cooled off, tell me how I can help you."*

*The two glasses of iced tea were gone in the blink of an eye. They each downed their cool drink with heads tilted back, eyes closed, and Adam's apples bobbing. While they guzzled their refreshing tea, I let my thumb do a soothing slide across each of their knee caps, just to make them feel more at home.*

*Still smacking their lips, and in perfect unison, they each leaned forward and placed their empty glasses on the coffee table to either side of me. When they did, I could smell the sweet scent of young, heated bodies. As anyone who has ever experienced the scent knows, it is the headiest scent known to man. And the most delicious.*

*Simply because I couldn't stop myself, I reached out to the Hispanic boy and tapped away an errant drop of iced tea that had lost its way and gone slithering down the side of his neck. The young black man turned to watch what I was doing, and he spotted another escaped drop of iced tea on the other side of his fellow's neck. So being a nice person and a friend, he wiped it away with a fingertip just as I had done.*

*The young man who was the center of our attentions, suddenly finding himself with our two sets of fingers on his overheated skin, gave a teeny sigh and leaned back into the cushions with eyes closed and a heavenly smile twisting his lips.*

*"That feels good," he muttered, seemingly to himself although I fear it was not.*

*The other young man darted smiling eyes in my direction. A quizzical expression crossed his dark face, and then he turned back to his mate and slid his hand into the vee of the young Hispanic's white shirt. With a flick of his thumb, he undid the top button of his friend's shirt to give his exploring hand more room. I thought it polite to lend a hand as well, so I reached out with both hands and tugged open the belts of both young men, just in case they were still not quite comfortable enough, don't you know? The Hispanic lad turned his head and laid his lips to the mouth of his companion. They each lifted their hips when I flicked open the button of their trousers and slid their zippers down in tandem. The Bibles, I noticed, were lying to either side, forgotten.*

*My two guests were lost in their kiss, so I took the opportunity and clutched a fistful of trouser material from each of them and tugged their pants down over their lovely young legs until they were dragged entirely away, after which I tossed the two pairs of trousers over my shoulders, where I heard them clatter to the floor—coins, cell phones, the lot.*

*Each lad was now down to white boxer shorts and a white shirt. The four lovely young legs before me were mouth-wateringly beautiful. Two black and two brown.*

*Stiff protuberances poking up the fabric of the two pairs of boxer shorts seemed to beg for assistance in their escape, so I took a grip on the legs of both pair of underwear and tugged them slowly down those four gorgeous young legs until they were out of the way. I flung the boxer shorts in the same direction I had flung the trousers. They landed considerably more quietly than the trousers had, with just a gentle hush of fabric.*

*Not that I cared.*

*Two dicks, one just as perfect and just as erect as the other, were my reward for this daring escapade, and I couldn't have been more pleased with myself if I had found a thousand-dollar bill on my front doorstep.*

The boys' kiss was becoming more heated, and their hands began exploring each other's torsos. Considerably freer now that their pants and shorts had been stripped away, my two young guests began writhing happily in their newfound freedom. With my pulse thundering contentedly in my ears, I leaned forward and took the young black man's dick into my mouth. When he gasped and clutched my hair, I eased his delicious cock from my mouth and tasted the young Hispanic for a change.

Both young men had pulled their lips from each other and were now watching me with eager expectation. As they unbuttoned their only remaining article of clothing to expose their smooth heaving chests, I let my hands range over each of them as I took turns tasting first one and then the other.

Being polite, as most Jehovah's witnesses are, they took pity on me and slid even closer together on the couch, leaning in toward each other so that their cocks were touching. By that incredible act of camaraderie, and with the two erections nestled one against the other, I found myself capable of sipping the precome from both youthful cocks simultaneously.

As I kneaded and stroked their warm chests, occasionally shifting my attentions to their tight ball sacs, which they seemed to enjoy considerably, I scooped both delicious cocks into my mouth at the same time and really went to town. Before long, four young legs were trembling and twitching at either side of me, and two young sets of lean hips were rising and falling and rising and falling as my tongue dragged a hymn from their sweet dicks.

"Oh, Jesus," someone muttered.

"Oh, Mother of God," another gasped.

And just as I began to hear the Hallelujah Chorus in the back of my own mind, each lad took a grip on one of my ears, and moving as one, they lifted their hips to cram their dicks as far down my throat as they would go.

The release of two hot streams of come made my eyes bulge open, but I rode out the storm like a pro. As the two

*Jehovah's Witnesses bucked and bounced and arched their backs into my ministrations with unbridled enthusiasm, I savored and sucked and swallowed every last drop of delicious young come that made its way between my lips.*

*Even when my two guests had emptied themselves out completely, at least for the moment, they held me there before them, still relishing the feel of my hot mouth on their tender cocks. And since I was hoping for another deluge of hot youthful man juice to make me smile yet again and bring more God into my heart, I didn't mind the extra work at all.*

*Twenty minutes later, when my guests had pulled themselves together, thanked me profusely, and downed another glass of tea to replenish lost juices, hee-hee-hee-hee, I stood at my door and watched them step back into the California heat, knowing I had done my best to give them an interlude of peace they would not soon forget.*

*With a smile and a final good-bye, I waved farewell to my two new friends. Turning back to my no-longer-boring and humdrum afternoon, I gazed down at the stack of Jehovah's Witness pamphlets they had thrust into my hands as they were leaving.*

*"Thank you, God," I said to the ceiling. "If I wasn't a believer before, I certainly am now."*

*If God deigned to answer, he must have done it in his head. I didn't hear a word.*

I WATCHED Arthur politely close the door in the faces of the two young Jehovah's Witnesses standing on the front porch. Only then did he turn back to me.

He gave me a cockeyed glare, part amusement, part disgust. He jerked a thumb at the two handsome chaps we could still hear retreating down the front steps.

"Beautiful, weren't they?" Arthur asked. "No doubt you would have asked them in."

I tried to give a convincing shrug. "I don't know what you're talking about."

"Yeah, right."

Before the doorbell rang, we had been standing in front of the fireplace in the living room, gazing at our reflections in the mirror over the mantle. It was high noon, a white-hot California sun was streaming through the windows, and the fireplace mirror, as always, was the most unflattering fucking mirror in the house.

Arthur picked up our conversation where the doorbell had killed it dead.

"But you're sixty-four years old!"

"Exactly my point, Arthur. Nobody needs a facelift when they're twenty."

"You don't need one *now!*"

"It's not like we can't afford it," I whined. Yes, I did. I admit it. I whined.

Arthur laughed. "And how long do you think it will take you to recover from a surgery like that? You're not young."

"So you keep saying," I snarled.

He huffed with impatience as he ignored my comment. "*And* you took forever to recover from the cataract surgery. Remember that? A facelift would be far more invasive. Hell, David, you might *never* recover."

"I'll never recover if I have to keep staring in the mirror at this baggy-ass face every day for the rest of my life."

"Don't be petulant. I, for one, happen to love your baggy-ass face."

I turned and stared at him with gaping mouth and eyes as big as pancakes. I know they were as big as pancakes because I could see them in that fucking mirror. "You really know how to hurt a guy."

"It was a wee jest. Lighten up, David. And stop talking about a facelift. Grow old gracefully, like me."

I narrowed my eyes so near to closed I barely had room to squeeze a glare through them. "Yes, with your banana facials, your weekly massages, your ninety-dollar haircuts, and the fact that I haven't seen you wear the same shirt twice in a row for over two years."

He shrugged. "I like all those things. They make me feel better about myself."

"A facelift would make me feel better about *myself.*"

"And what if you came out of it looking like Bruce Jenner or Mickey Rourke, God forbid. They both look like a couple of monkeys someone wrung out like dishrags. Or Jennifer Grey. What about her?"

"Jennifer Grey looks fabulous!"

"Yes, and she also looks like a totally different person. Killed her career dead. Even her friends didn't recognize her afterward. Her own father wouldn't give her an autograph."

"I don't have a career to worry about. Remember? And not too many friends either. And certainly nobody begging for autographs."

"Maybe not, but you don't want to look like a stranger, do you? It has taken me forty years to get used to the way you look. I'd hate to have to break in another you."

I blinked. "It took you forty years to get used to the way I look?"

Arthur laughed and pulled me into his arms. "That was another wee joke, dearest." I tried to wiggle free but he wouldn't let me go. "I love the way you look. I have loved the way you look since the first day I met you. I loved the way you looked this morning when you stumbled out of bed cussing the cat because you woke up with its ass in your face. And I loved the way you looked every day in between. Please don't change yourself, David. Please don't become somebody you aren't. Not for vanity. Please. Not for that."

I finally squirmed out of his embrace, although a bit more gently, and resumed the perusal of my face in the damned mirror. While he watched with his head still on my shoulder, I tapped the side of my temple with a fingertip as if checking the consistency of a bowl of pudding. "How about a few shots of Botox? How would you feel about me doing that?"

"Then you'd look like Thomas Jefferson on Mount Rushmore. Seen Jefferson smile lately? No, David, you haven't. That's because his face is made of stone. And if you pump yourself full of Botox, *your* face will be made of stone too. Expressionless. I don't want you expressionless. I would miss those glares of pure outrage when I get to the New York Times crossword puzzle before you do. And I would really miss the way you squeeze your eyes shut and your mouth flies open every time you scream your way through an orgasm."

"I don't scream," I said, fighting back a smile.

"Oh, please. When was the last time you came quietly?"

"Yesterday morning when I jacked off in the bathroom and didn't want you to hear."

"What did you do? Stuff a towel in your mouth?"

"Pretty much," I said, as a giggle fell out. It was a surprise giggle. I had no idea it was anywhere near.

Arthur coughed up a giggle of his own to meet it and shake its hand. "So no facelift. All right?"

I molded my face into a perfect replica of disenchantment, which, had I been loaded with Botox would most certainly have been impossible, just as Arthur conjectured.

"For now," I conceded. "But the first time I trip on my jowls navigating the front steps it's under the knife I go."

He gave me a snarky grin. "Just watch where you're walking."

"Prick," I said.

"Shitheel," he answered.

We both turned to gaze at our side-by-side reflections in the mirror. Arthur was still an inch or so taller than me. His eyes were still as blue as the Mediterranean Sea. His ginger-blond hair was still lightened with gray, but subtly, as if it was intentionally put there.

Arthur was still perfect.

Standing beside his beauty, I looked like I had just crawled from the crypt. Or so I imagined. Arthur apparently didn't share my opinion.

He reached out and touched the mirror, right where my reflected nose was. His soft blue eyes were filled with love as he gazed at me. "The way you are is exactly the way I want you. It will shatter my old heart into a billion bits if you change yourself even one little whit, David Ayres."

"Then we'd have to get you a new heart," I said, smiling gently at the man I had loved so long, and who had loved me back for just as long in return.

"No," he said. "I like the heart I have. And I like the man it's filled with."

His eyes opened wide in wonder, and he turned from the mirror to stare at *me* instead of my reflection. "You're blushing," he breathed. "Just like you did that day at the mission when we were sitting on the bench in the garden and I laid my hand on your knee. It was the first time we ever touched. Do you remember?"

"Yes. I remember."

While he continued to stare at me, I turned my eyes away, returning to the mirror. "Have you ever regretted the life you've lived, Arthur? Have you ever wished there might have been more?"

Slowly, and sadly, his eyes followed mine to the mirror. His fingers stroked my nape. His voice was like far-off music, easy on the ear, soothing. "How could there have ever been more? I've spent my years with the love of my life. And in that life there has never been one sad day. Not one. Even when things went horribly wrong, I could turn and find peace and contentment knowing you were there beside me." He gave a self-deprecating chuckle. "I'm sixty-one years old, and I still get hard seeing you dress. When I wake up to the smell of your sleep-warm skin in the morning, it makes me tremble just as it did when I was twenty-one. I think of you a hundred times a day, and every time I do, I thank God you're part of my life. No. Not part of my life. You're *all* of my life, David. Every thread, stitch, and ribbon of it. I can't imagine what the last forty years would have been like without you. And it's something I *never* want to imagine."

His speech was so unexpected and so filled with truth and passion, it left me breathless.

"Thank you, Arthur" was all I could think to say.

And when Arthur *realized* it was all I could think to say, a shadow of hurt darkened his eyes. He looked down at the wedding ring on his finger, then back at his own reflection in the mirror, studiously ignoring me completely.

I opened my mouth to speak, to say something more romantic than what I had blurted out, but I knew it was too late. The moment was lost.

Arthur ran a hand along the ledge in front of us. "I'll tell the maid to be a little more industrious in her dusting, shall I, then? We don't want to live in a pigsty, after all."

And with that, he turned and walked away.

"I love you," I said to his retreating back.

To which he replied without turning, and without stopping, "I know you do, David. But maybe just not enough."


ARTHUR AND I settled into my little Hillcrest apartment, and it was the happiest time of my life.

It was also the saddest, for I quickly learned that unspoken words are not the only things that hover. Ninety-day visas can hover too. And they are far more threatening than words when they do.

The thought of Arthur being torn from my arms over a matter of bureaucratic red tape was almost too much to bear. But little did I know that Arthur was all over our little dilemma. He had it covered. While I was most certainly crazy about the guy and couldn't get him out of my head for more than five seconds at a stretch, even *if* the L-word had yet to be uttered by either of us, I had also underevaluated Arthur's stubborn refusal to accept any sort of lifestyle which he did not fully embrace.

And apparently, he flatly refused to accept any lifestyle that didn't have me in it.

While Arthur's mother and father lived in Liverpool, a once booming English city of half a million souls in the County of Lancashire, situated on the eastern side of the Mersey Estuary, or so Arthur told me, they were also in residence there less than one or two months out of the year. Arthur's parents traveled. And that is almost all they did.

Arthur's father and mother had built a clothing empire that, by the time they started selling stock in it, earning themselves a hefty sum year after year after year, had traversed the globe. I tried on more than one occasion to coax the exact *amount* of that hefty sum from Arthur, but he would only tell me it was "several gazillion bob" and leave it at that. Since the company logo was—and is—known worldwide, and instantly recognizable by even the dimmest and least fashionable bulb on the planet, I could pretty well imagine the figure Arthur was hinting at. While Arthur's parents no longer ruled this enterprise singlehandedly, as they had at its conception, they still parked themselves at the head of the table, side by side, on the company's board of directors. They were still, for all intents and purposes, in charge of the damn thing, since on a whim they could snap their collective fingers and heads would literally roll. Or so Arthur happily told me.

Unknown to me, as Arthur and I were imagining ourselves an old married couple in my tiny, one-bedroom garret apartment situated over the heads of two old queens who loved me like a son, and who were quickly coming to love Arthur as well, Arthur's own father was setting wheels in motion that would promise his only son the happiness, and stability, Arthur demanded.

On the dawn of the eighty-seventh day of the dratted ninety-day visa, I awoke as always in Arthur's arms. His naked, lean body against mine felt like heaven, all sleep-warm softness and hard edges. I was so used to the feel of him now that I could not imagine waking any other way. While we had still not spoken the L-word in each other's company, it was now on the tip of my tongue every waking moment.

It was all I could do to refrain from speaking it now.

John Inman

Arthur pressed his lips to the hollow of my throat and spoke the words that almost stopped my heart. "I'm leaving for England today."

I jerked out of his arms and leaped from the bed as if I had woken in flames.

"What are you saying? There's three days left!"

His eyes traveled over my naked body as I stood there trembling at the side of the bed. He patted the sheets beside him, his voice husky with sleep and desire. "Come back," he whispered. "Lay with me."

Already a tear had spilled from my eye. I angrily brushed it aside. I knew then that I had to speak the word. I had to. I swallowed a sob. My heart felt like an aching lump of lead, motionless and dead inside my chest.

"I won't let you go. I love you too much."

A gentle smile turned his mouth. "So you've finally said it, then."

"Yes!" I spat, a seething anger welling up inside me. "And I'll never not say it again. I won't let you go, Arthur. I won't!"

He rolled across the bed, sliding his naked body from beneath the sheet and exposing himself completely. The hair on his legs was golden in the dawning sunlight streaming through the window. The skin of his back was pale and unblemished. Faultless. The arm that reached out for me was beautifully shaped and blurred with a dusting of golden hair that perfectly matched his legs. The fingers of his hand grasped mine, and I didn't have the strength to pull away.

When he spoke, his voice was as soft as eider on the air. "Can I say it now too, David? Can I tell you I love you?"

He pulled me onto the bed, and I burrowed into his arms, my face damp with tears. He tucked the dampness against his chest, and I breathed in the scent of him. His fingers stroked my hair as he whispered against my ear.

"I love you too, David," he breathed. "You have to know that by now. And I'm not leaving. Not for long."

I hiccupped. "What do you mean?"

He tilted my head up so our eyes could meet. "What do you mean?" I said again. "Tell me."

"There is paperwork for me to sign. A green card is being issued, but I have to go to England to apply for it. My folks set it up. I'll be working for them in their West Coast headquarters here in San Diego. I've told them about you, David. And I told them I wouldn't leave you. This was the solution my mother came up with, and while Pops wasn't thrilled, he finally decided to go along. I guess they've given up on me growing out of this homo phase they thought I was going through. They've decided to let me live the life I'm determined to live. And alongside the person I want to live it with."

I swallowed another sob. "Me?"

Arthur grinned. "No. Walter Cronkite. Yes, dumbass. You."

I pulled him closer, burying my fingers in his ginger hair. "And you swear you'll come back?"

He laughed then, even as his tongue came out and licked a tear from my cheek. "Hmm. Delicious. And yes. I'll come back. And when I do, I'll be a grossly overpaid employee of Mum and Pop's little global empire. A *teeny* empire," he conceded, "but an empire nevertheless. Happily for me, being the one and only fruit of their withered loins, I won't even have to fret about quarterly evaluations. We're set for life, baby. All I have to do is not run the Colonial end of the company into the ground. I think I can handle that. I told Pop he could have it one way or the other. I could be a useless drain on his old age, never working a day and being an endless pain in the ass and asking for more money every minute of every fucking day. Or I could hitch up my pants and help him run the business. He didn't get where he is by not knowing a good deal when he hears one. I could have drained the coffers quite easily if he hadn't agreed."

I finally found a smile inside me and offered it up for inspection. "I'm sure you could. I've seen you shop."

An odd silence fell over us as, once again, I let the heavenly heat of his naked body soak through me. His breath was sleep sweet and warm on my skin. His leg folded over my waist held me in a scissor hold I couldn't have escaped from even had I wanted to. Which I sure as hell didn't.

"So we're lovers, then," I said. "We're really—lovers."

He rested his hand against my cheek. His thumb brushed another tear away. "For as long as you'll have me," he said. "For as long as you'll love me back."

I laid my ear to his chest to better hear the pounding of his heart. I loved the sound of it beating there. So strong. So close. So mine.

"I'll always love you back, Arthur. Always."

And when our lips came together, it felt like going home.

"You're mine," I whispered into the kiss. "You're really mine."

"Forever," he softly said as his hands began to move.

# Chapter Four

THE GARDENER'S name was Jaime. He was Mexican, in his early twenties, probably illegal, and absolutely gorgeous. With skin the color of cherrywood, deep brown eyes almost lost behind long, dark, fluttering eyelashes, and a mouthful of the whitest teeth I had ever seen in my life, it was all I could do not to drop everything and simply sit around staring at him every time he showed up to care for the lawn. Jaime's English was every bit as good as my Spanish, and my Spanish was nonexistent.

Today he was trimming and treating the grapevines that grew up the west side of the house from ground to eaves. As luck would have it, on this day the temperature was nudging up to the ninety-degree mark, and Jaime—thank you, God—had removed his shirt to work...

*...WHILE I found imaginary chores to do at the kitchen sink, where I could stare out at him like the old lech I truly was. Arthur was out running, so I didn't even have to pretend to be doing something else. Every ounce of my concentration could be centered on the astonishing spectacle of Jaime's bare torso flexing and bending as he stood on the ladder by the kitchen window and worked on the vines. Occasionally he would duck his head, peer through the window, and flash those stunning white teeth in my direction, just to be polite.*

*I loved it when Jaime was polite.*

*His grass-strewn trousers seemed to be a couple of sizes too large. As he perched on the ladder directly in front of the kitchen window I saw they sagged most welcomingly over the swell of his ass, the skin color of which, while not as dark as Jaime's back, was still a muted bronze. It was, in truth, one of the most fetching asses I had ever seen in my life. Smooth, firm, bubbled, and with a teeny sprouting of dark hair sprinkling the skin at the base of his spine where the two mounds joined.*

*Even more enticing than the posterior view of Jaime's sagging trousers, was the anterior view. With his Dickies clinging precariously to his slender hip bones, a wondrous expanse of flat belly and a broad veldt of black pubic hair peeked out above the waistband to draw my eye and make my saliva positively gush. Occasionally, and Lord I loved it when this happened, as Jaime stood on the ladder smack in front of my vantage point at the kitchen sink, he would dip a few fingers beneath his waistband in the front and stir the hair there as if he had an itch.*

*Rest assured, when Jaime itched, I itched. Although mine, I fear, was a different sort of itch.*

*I was just about to do my June Cleaver routine and run out the side door with a cold bottle of soda pop for my hard-working gardener, just to be nice, when I heard a sudden "Aaiiee!" and the next thing I knew, Jaime was lying on the lawn at the foot of the kitchen window, flat on his back and gasping for air like a grounded trout.*

*I sailed through the kitchen door. In my terror, I fear, I was gasping almost as much as he was.*

*I dropped to my knees beside the poor man and laid my hand on the heat of his stomach, just to show concern.*

*"Jaime, you fell."*

*I could see the air was knocked out of him. Since he couldn't quite speak yet, he simply eyeballed me with those wide, gorgeous eyes and made a perfect little O with his mouth, which even now I could barely drag my eyes from.*

*Well, that's not true. It was his crotch I couldn't drag my eyes from. Somehow during the course of the fall, Jaime almost managed to lose his trousers altogether. As he lay on his back on my side lawn, gasping for air, they were now so precariously hanging on to his hips that a truly wide expanse of pubic hair was exposed, not to mention the base of what looked to be an extremely lovely dick nestled in the middle of it.*

*My fingers may have slipped from his stomach just far enough to brush that lovely patch of pubes. I'm not sure. Well, yes I am. They did. And I'm not sorry. Not in the least little bit. But even more to the point, Jaime didn't seem sorry either.*

*He blinked his eyes a few times when my fingers ducked into the shrubbery of his crotch, just to get out of the sun, you know, and believe it or not, a teeny smile exposed his snow white teeth for my viewing enjoyment. He seemed to be catching his breath.*

*He laid a hand over mine and smiled all the wider.*

*I glanced around. We were quite alone, protected by the house on one side, the garden fence on all the other sides, and the shade of our old sycamore tree shielding us from above. We couldn't have been more secluded if we had been stranded on a desert isle. And what a lovely thought that was.*

*I could have moved my hand from his stomach, but I didn't. I could have done a lot of things I didn't.*

*What I did do was rustle Jaime's patch of pubic hair a bit more briskly with my fingertips, and lo and behold, the base of his cock, which was still slightly exposed beneath the edge of his waistband, appeared to swell up like a bullfrog.*

*Now it was my turn to blink. When the front of Jaime's trousers began to tent, I blinked again.*

*"Can you sit up?" I asked.*

*And to my infinite delight, he grinned. His hand, which had been resting over mine, slid a little to the south and flipped the button on the top of his trousers. The moment it did, his cock bobbed and weaved and slid from its fabric prison, seeking the light of day.*

*Now it was my turn to smile. "I guess you're okay, then, are you? Breathe better now, can you, with that nasty button out of the way?"*

*He nodded and peered away from my face to stare at his crotch. Then he peered back at me.*

*Since my patient seemed to be improving from one moment to the next, I thought I should continue the course of treatment I had already embarked upon. So I dipped my hand beneath his waistband and circled his dick with my fingertips.*

*Jaime closed his eyes and stretched his back into a tiny arch to meet my touch. By that I assumed his spine was undamaged. The prognosis was getting better all the time.*

*When I slid my fingertips around the sheath of his uncircumcised cock and slid the heated foreskin downward out of the way, his smile broadened. By this I knew he had suffered no numbness of his lower extremities in the fall. As any doctor in the world will tell you, that is good news for certain.*

*Sitting in the grass beside him, I gave Jaime a little wink, as if asking for directions, and he gave me a little wink back as if to say, "Señor, you know the road you want to take as well as I do."*

*And I did indeed.*

*So with my free hand I tugged Jaime's trousers just a little farther down his hips and out of the way, exposing two lovely hairy thighs. But it wasn't the thighs I was concerned with at the moment. For by pushing the trousers completely out of the way, I had exposed Jaime's dick and balls to the afternoon air. The only protection from the elements they could boast of now was the fact that the whole delicious package was resting in my hand.*

*Again he gave me a wink and arched his back a little farther into my touch. By this I knew he was making perfect sense, doing what anybody would have done under similar circumstances, and in this way I deduced he had suffered no concussion or other sort of brain damage in his fall. This was really, really, really good news. Medically speaking.*

*To celebrate, I dipped my head and slipped my lips over the head of his dick, and once I had explored the terrain with my tongue for a moment, glans, slit, the whole shebang—just to be polite and not rush things—I decided to go whole hog and take that delicious dick all the way in.*

*When I did, Jaime gave a delectable grunt, gripped the back of my head with his gloved hand (yes, he was still wearing his gloves), and again thrust his hips in my direction. Not once, but several times. Over and over and over.*

*Had I won the lottery, I couldn't have been happier.*

*I cupped Jaime's hot balls in my hand as I continued to slurp away at his wonderful cock, and the moment his back gave an arch that would have splintered the spine of a lesser creature, I knew I had cured my patient completely.*

*"Oh oh oh oh o-o-o-oh!" he gasped, and the next thing I knew my mouth was filled with a delicious explosion of hot, tasty come, fresh from the manufacturer. Jaime thumped his hips into my face like a jackhammer, and every time he did, another squirt of jism slapped the roof of my mouth, or ran down my throat, or dribbled out the side of my lips.*

*"One more," I pleaded inside my head. "Please, Jaime, just one more!"*

*And as if he could hear my thoughts, he tore at my hair with his clenched fist and stabbed his cock one more time into the back of my throat, where it unleashed a final squirt of hot semen.*

*When his thrusts began to weaken, he finally managed to close his gasping mouth, and just to show he was a nice guy, he released his death grip on my hair, which in another moment or two would have undoubtedly rendered me bald.*

*Not that I minded.*

*I pulled my mouth from around his dick, licked my lips with what I'm sure was a smugly satisfied expression on my face, and bent my head one last time to kiss Jaime's lovely tummy. He patted my head when I did. Mexicans are such a friendly race.*

*He raised himself onto his elbows. "Gracias, Meester Ayres."*

*"Thank you, Jaime."*

*He blessed me with a resplendent smile, and I groaned my way to my feet. A moment later he groaned his way to his.*

*"Back to work, then, I suppose," I muttered happily. "And be careful on that ladder."*

*He bobbed his handsome head up and down a few times to show he agreed. His teeth flashed white in the sun. He wiped a hand across his chest, dispersing a film of sweat and perhaps a few splatters of come.*

*I studied his beauty for one second longer, sighed deeply, then rested a hand on his shoulder to give it a gentle squeeze before heading back to the house.*

*And all the while he watched me go, that resplendent smile never left his face.*

I blinked the fantasy away and stared out at Jaime as he trimmed the hedges by the kitchen window. The sun was high and hot, and his strong young shoulders were baked to the color of hazelnuts. The clean line leading down from the nape of his neck to the flare of those wonderful shoulders drew my eye every time. A pool of moisture always settled into the small of his back on days like this, darkening the little tuft of hair at the base of his spine. In my opinion, he truly was one of the most beautiful men I had ever seen.

His heart-stopping smile lit up like a beacon when he glanced up and saw me standing at the window watching him. He brushed the sweat from his forehead with the back of a gloved hand and then proceeded to lay that hand against the window glass in way of greeting. I laid my hand against his on the other side of the pane. Then each of us turned away to go back to what we were doing before. Me with a sigh, Jaime with a renewed look of concentration.

I had been secretly nuts about Jaime since he came to work for us six years ago, when the arthritis in my knees limited the gardening I loved, making it hard for me to do some of the more difficult tasks of keeping the property looking groomed. Sometimes, when the work he needed to do was particularly heavy or time consuming, he would bring his brother along to help him out. His brother was just as handsome and just as kind as Jaime. I often wished I could follow them home one day, simply to get a glimpse of the sort of life they lived in Tijuana. They must have been happy there. No two young men could be so contented in their souls if they were miserable at home. Were they married? Did they have children? Did the American dollars I paid the two of them make their lives a little easier? A little less desperate?

I suspected this was the case, if for no other reason than the fact that neither brother ever treated me or Arthur with anything less that respect and affection. *True* affection. The trueness of it was right there in those heavenly brown eyes, crystal clear and piercing. It had never faded in all the years we had known them. Never once.

As I tried to tear my attention from Jaime's lovely lithe body standing outside the kitchen window, I was helped along by a couple of pale arms suddenly materializing out of nowhere and wrapping themselves around my waist from behind.

I dropped the dish towel I was holding and reached out quickly to close the curtain window above the sink.

Arthur giggled with his lips to the back of my neck. "Don't be a prude, David. Let's show our little gardener friend what true love really looks like."

I wiggled around in Arthur's grasp until we were face to face. "Arthur, I find it hard to believe that anyone who looks like Jaime doesn't already know exactly what love really looks like. He must have the señoritas falling all over themselves to get into his pants."

One roaming eyebrow climbed toward Arthur's hairline. "Not unlike yourself, I'm afraid."

I could feel a blush rising to my cheeks, but I ignored it. "Oh, don't be silly. I'm old enough to be his father."

Arthur clucked his tongue. "Grandfather, actually. You and me both."

"Thanks," I said. "That makes me feel so much better."

Arthur laughed. He pulled me into his arms a little tighter. His lips were on my ear when he said, "Are you still angry?"

"I wasn't the one who was angry, Arthur. You were."

"Was I?"

"Yes. Don't you remember? You thought I was cruising the jogger, and the priest, and the Jehovah's Witnesses and the—"

"Oh, that. Yes, I do remember now. At least I think I do. I seem to be...." His sentence trailed away as his hand came up to brush my gray hair back away from my face.

"You seem to be what?"

He ignored the question, still studying my hair. "You need a haircut."

"I know."

"I'll cut it for you, David. You used to let me."

"I know. But it's silly for you to go to all that trouble. It's far easier to stop by the barber on the way to the store."

"But I liked cutting your hair."

I eased out of his arms, and when I did, I saw the happy glimmer in his eyes fade.

"Make love to me," Arthur said. "Or let me make love to you."

I gave up a weary groan. "I have so much to do right now. And the gardener's here. What if he wants to ask a question in the middle of us bonking on the kitchen floor?"

Arthur's hand slipped over my crotch, and I have to admit I felt a thrill when it did. "What a marvelous idea. Bonking on the kitchen floor." He waved a hand across the Marmoleum at his feet. "Care to join me, my love? Just an afternoon quickie. Nothing to be afraid of. I'll even close the rest of the kitchen curtains if you're feeling prudish."

For some reason I stubbornly ignored that glimmer of a thrill Arthur's touch had just given me. I pushed it away instead. Just as I pushed away his hand.

I laid my hand over his cheek and gave him a paternal peck on the cheek. "Later, Arthur. We'll have a date night later. All right?"

He brushed a hand across the fly of his trousers and I saw that he was excited. He looked down at me and saw that I was not.

With one last piercing gaze of his azure eyes, he forced a look of resignation onto his face and reached up to give my hair a tousle. "Later, then," he said. He glanced at his watch. "That will give you about ten hours to think of another excuse."

"Arthur—"

"I'm going running. I'll see you later."

And he was gone.

I turned back to the window and slid the curtains aside. Jaime was gone as well. Working on the other side of the house, perhaps.

I sighed and went back to drying the dishes.


AS ARTHUR and I set up housekeeping in my tiny walk-up apartment, Arthur focused every ounce of his energy on becoming American. Well, not every ounce. He also focused a goodly portion of his heart and soul and time and commitment to becoming a lover he thought I would be proud of. It was, of course, a considerable waste of his energies since I couldn't have been more proud of him anyway.

Nor could I have loved him more. Arthur's love for me, and mine for him, were as solid on the air around us as the scent of Mr. B's roses wafting through the apartment window. And with no doubts whatsoever holding us back, we committed ourselves to each other completely.

Put bluntly, neither of us had ever been happier.

With his green card in perfect working order, and both our career paths now moving along swimmingly (he managing the American side of his family's business and me climbing my way slowly up the corporate ranks of the bank where I worked in downtown San Diego) our lives fell into a beautiful and precise pattern.

The L-word was freely spoken now. Freely spoken and truly felt. Thanks to our two jobs (and Arthur's wealthy family), we had no financial worries at all. We could have easily afforded a larger living space, but we kept our tiny garret apartment in the fine old Craftsman home in Hillcrest because Mr. B and Mr. C had become more than landlords. They had become friends.

In the two years since Arthur first climbed the steps to my little apartment, a continent away from where he was born and raised, the health of Mr. B and Mr. C had failed considerably. It was hardly noticeable at first, but soon even Arthur and I, in our own busy lives, could not ignore what was happening directly beneath us.

So we stayed. And gradually, as time passed, we helped Mr. B and Mr. C conquer the difficulties of old age without them being forced to resort to charity from strangers. They were proud men, and they were accomplished men. Their minds were still vibrant. Only their bodies had fallen behind in the long race of life.

It seemed odd that, as they had done everything together during their many long years as a couple, their health began to fail in unison as well.

Mr. C explained it to me once by saying they had become mirror images of each other. What one image did, the other reflected. I thought I had never heard love defined more perfectly.

To celebrate Arthur's and my second anniversary together, Mr. B and Mr. C invited us downstairs to the main house for dinner.

They pulled out all the stops. Their finest crystal and polished silver surrounded china they had purchased in the Orient many long years before on one of their worldly jaunts. The table linen, they said, hailed from another trip. That one to Ireland.

Dinner was catered, for neither man did much cooking anymore. After we tore into the rack of lamb and curried potatoes like four mongrel dogs who hadn't eaten in a month, Mr. B and Mr. C directed us to the living room, where we found a fire lit in the fireplace, even though it was the dead of summer.

Arthur and I sat hand in hand, sipping Drambuie from fine old snifters and listening to our hosts tell of an especially exciting trip they had taken to South Africa many years earlier. Ceiling fans hummed above our heads, dispensing the summer warmth and the heat from the fire. Through the open window leading out to the garden, I heard the ratcheting of crickets, smelled the ever-present scent of roses. The liqueur sent a mellow heat through my body, and what heat the drink did not produce, Arthur's nearness did.

When the hour grew late, the stories petered out, and Mr. B and Mr. C leaned in from their leather chairs by the fire and settled sweet smiles on the two of us sitting there before them.

Mr. C cleared his throat when he saw they had our full attention. "We're leaving it all to you, boys. The house. The bank accounts. Everything."

Arthur and I were stunned. "But, wait," Arthur said, setting his drink aside and gripping my hand a little tighter. "Don't you have family? Surely one of you must have relatives—"

Mr. B gave his old head an impatient shake. "Our families turned their backs on us the day we found each other. As far as we're concerned, the only family we have left is sitting in this very room. You boys are our family. And we want to take care of you."

"I don't know what to say," I stammered.

But Arthur said it better. He clutched his chest with the hand that was not in mine and smiled at the two gentlemen as he patted his heart. "We are honored. But there are long years to wait before we'll be spending your money. Hell, you two will probably outlive David and me."

"If you say so," Mr. B intoned with a secretive gleam in his eye.

Mr. C then clapped his hands, signaling the evening was over.

Arthur and I downed the last of our drinks, and after many thanks and many hugs, we wended our way out the open doors leading into the rose garden and, arm in arm, we headed up the stairs to our tiny apartment.

The next morning on my way to work, I stopped by the kitchen window to tap a good-bye to our two old friends, who were always there at this time having breakfast.

But today they were nowhere in sight.

Concerned, I knocked at the door, and when no one answered, I tried the knob. It was unlocked.

I stepped into the kitchen and gazed around. The leftover food from the dinner party was still wrapped in foil on the countertop. In the dining room, I found the dinner table still set with the dirty dishes from dinner. The house smelled of ashes and I ducked into the living room to find the fire in the fireplace had burnt out, and our four brandy glasses were still scattered about the room where everyone had left them.

"Mr. B! Mr. C!" I called out at the foot of the teak staircase leading up to their bedroom. "Are you all right?"

I had never heard the house so silent.

My feet were leaden as I dragged myself up the staircase. I did not call their names again. Somehow I knew they would not answer if I did.

At the end of the long hallway leading to the opposite end of the house from where our apartment was situated, and walled off separately, I saw the old gentlemen's bedroom door standing ajar. Through the opening, only silence leaked out into the hall.

The hallway seemed a mile long as I forced myself to walk it, every step taking me closer to that partially opened door and what I already knew lay behind it.

Finally, I reached my destination, and sucking in a steadying gulp of air, I gently pushed the door inward.

The antique four-poster bed was still perfectly made. Atop the quilt with the lavender primroses sewed into it, lay Mr. B and Mr. C, hand in hand, curled toward each other in death. They were wearing the same clothes they had worn at dinner.

On the nightstand beside the bed sat an empty bottle of pills.

Looking closer, I saw that the two men's faces were only inches apart. Their four hands clasped together beneath their chins.

They were smiling the same smiles they had worn in life. Then, as now, their smiles were only for each other.

I SLIPPED Arthur's suit jacket off his shoulders, and rather than let it slide to the floor, I carefully folded it and placed it over the back of a chair. Once that chore was accomplished, I loosened my tie, kicked off my shoes, and headed for the kitchen to pour myself a drink.

After two years together, Arthur knew me as well as I knew myself. At my back he said, "Pour one for me too, ducks. Funerals make me thirsty."

It had been a rough three days. And even with Mr. B and Mr. C safely tucked into a hillside beneath a eucalyptus tree, one atop the other in a single plot at Mount Hope Cemetery, just off the 94 freeway, Arthur and I could still not believe everything that had happened.

Three days ago we were paying rent on a tiny walk-up apartment, which admittedly we both loved for the sheer reason that we had each other in it, and now we not only owned the apartment, but we also owned the house and property around it.

Mr. B and Mr. C had been true to their word. In fact, according to their attorney, a gentleman not much younger than they were, the two men had settled their will with Arthur and me as heirs almost six months before that final dinner party, when they told us what they had done.

How long had they been planning their suicides, we wondered? How long had they known that old age was progressively robbing them of more and more of their happiness and one day would take a massive step forward and rob one of them of the other for all time, leaving the survivor all alone in a world where he was not accustomed to being alone at all?

Was it that fear, that fear of being left alone, that finally convinced them to do what they had done? To not wait for death to set the date for them, but to set the date themselves? Was the fear of dying less terrifying for the two men knowing they would not travel the road alone? Did they snuff their candles happily, knowing they would take that one final journey together, hand in hand, just as they had journeyed the living world for all the long years they had been together?

I served Arthur his scotch, and he immediately raised it in a toast. "To Mr. B and Mr. C. Thank you, good friends, and may you rest together in peace."

I nodded and echoed, "Thank you."

Our glasses clinked, and we took a long pull of scotch before we walked into each other's arms.

"Make love to me," Arthur whispered against my ear. "Please, David. I love you so much. Make love to me now. I need to feel you against me."

I plucked his glass from his hand and set both glasses on the kitchen counter. Cradling his face with my fingertips, I stared deep into his eyes as I laid my lips over his. I only broke the kiss to say, "Come with me." And I led him by the hand to the bedroom.

The bed was still unmade after we had rushed out to attend the funeral. I yanked the disheveled mound of sheets and blankets off it completely, tossing them into the corner. With the bed bare and waiting, I pulled at my clothes as Arthur did the same with his. In less than a minute, we were naked, and only then did we once again walk into each other's arms.

Arthur's skin was a familiar road. I knew every inch of him now. He knew every inch of me. The heat and texture of his body never ceased to amaze me. When his strong arms scooped me against his chest in a massive hug and his hardening cock pressed snug against my own, I let myself melt into his embrace.

He eased me down onto the bed and crouched over me, dragging his mouth from my lips to the hollow in my throat, where he laid claim with a flick of his tongue. As he kissed me, he reached over to the nightstand and pulled open a drawer.

He rose up onto his knees, still straddling and hovering over me, and poured lotion into his hand. While he did that, I slipped my own hand around his cock and made him tremble as I pushed back his foreskin to expose him completely. I dampened my fingers with my own saliva and slid them over the head of his dick until I felt him shudder. Then he shuddered again as he laid his lotion-coated fingertips against his own opening and moistened himself for me.

It was my turn to shudder when Arthur spread the remaining lotion over my erect cock, and as his mouth once again found mine, he lowered himself onto me, slowly at first, and then, as if he couldn't wait any longer, he forced himself down onto me until he opened for me completely. Somewhere between agony and paradise, I felt my cock tear into him as far as it could go. With my pubic hair scraping his hole, he gasped out a laugh of sheer bliss, and his tongue worked its way into our kiss.

I sucked on his tongue as he began moving over me. I arched my hips to meet every rise of his, scared to death he would pull away completely. But he never did.

I stroked his warm back as his ass continued to engulf me, the heat of it enough to continually bring my knees up off the bed in sheer ecstasy. With every third or fourth stroke, he would force himself down onto me even harder so that my dick would bury itself as far into him as he could get it. Every one of those strokes made me gasp for air.

The minutes passed. Our movements became less controlled. I was close to coming deep inside him when he pulled away from our kiss and locked his eyes to mine.

"Never leave me, David. I love you so much. Please tell me you'll never leave me."

I gripped his hips and forced his ass back down over my cock because I simply couldn't bear not to feel him around me completely. I pulled his face down to mine and smothered it with kisses.

"You know I'll never leave you. You're mine forever. You promised me you were, and I'm going to hold you to that promise." I arched my back higher, once again burying my cock deep inside this man I loved so much.

"Come for me," Arthur groaned, his eyes finally blocking me from their beauty as he squeezed them shut at the sensation of my hardness piercing him all the way to his core. "Oh, come for me, baby, please."

I gripped his hair and pulled his mouth down onto mine once again, and as soon as I did, I felt my come shatter that excruciating wall of restraint that every man feels just before the moment of explosion. A heartbeat later my seed was spewing forth deep inside him.

"I can feel it!" he cried. "I can feel you coming!"

He buried my own cries with a kiss, and it was then I felt his come spilling out across my stomach. We shuddered and bucked and gasped against each other as our bodies were drained of juices. The scent of semen filled the room. I longed to taste him, so I dipped my fingers in the come he had poured over me and carried it to my mouth, where I sucked it from my fingers like cream.

"Forever," he said again as his body slowly melted over me. Weary. Drained. Fulfilled.

"Forever," I whispered back. "It will always be you, Arthur. Always."

As our hearts slowed and the passion released us, we closed our eyes and held on for dear life.

Only later, when we had cleaned up and tossed back another couple of scotches, did we find the nerve to enter the main part of the house through the kitchen door at the foot of the stairs, down where Mr. B's roses still bobbed in the breeze by the garden fence. There we stepped inside the main house and laid claim to what, through the kindness of two elderly gentlemen who loved us like sons, truly now belonged to us.

Again, we raised our glasses. This time toasting the silence of the house.

The silence Mr. B and Mr. C had left for Arthur and me to fill.

IT WAS in Arthur's fifty-ninth year on the planet that the shareholders of the company he helmed here in the states took it upon themselves to vote him off the board of directors. Arthur's parents were long gone by then, of course. The company had gone public years earlier. Through judicious choices and hard work, Arthur had expanded the number of stores who now stocked the clothing his company made and, in doing so, had made his shareholders rich. He was still one of the major shareholders, but apparently even that was not enough to keep him at the helm.

We were both stunned when we learned he had been booted to the curb.

By this time I was Vice President of the bank where I had worked since I was just out of college. We were both well off beyond our wildest imaginings. So the moment we learned of Arthur's forced retirement, I chose to give up my job as well.

To counterbalance the sudden loss of work that had filled our lives for so many years, unbeknownst to me, Arthur devised a plan.

He unfolded the plan over breakfast one morning, just as the summer California heat had cooled to the balmy splendor of autumn. He unfolded it, yes, but not before I got my little dig in first. For wonder of wonders, Arthur had come to the breakfast table wearing a suit.

I couldn't believe it. "A suit? Why are you dressed for work, Arthur? You're unemployed now, remember? You're wearing the new tie I bought you for your last birthday and another new shirt I've never seen before. You're even wearing shoes. And at breakfast! What's up?"

"This," he said, extracting a tiny velvet box from his shirt pocket and sliding it across the table with a fingertip.

I picked up the box and stared at it. "And what, pray tell, *is* this?"

"Open it and see," he said with a mysterious glint in his eye.

So I did. Inside the velvet box sat two gold rings. Perfect, simple bands with only one decoration on each—a tiny gold bird, wings outstretched. The golden birds sat in the center of each band as if preparing for flight.

"These are beautiful," I breathed. "Where did you get them?"

Arthur gave me another of those sweet smiles that always unnerved me—and undressed me—almost every time one was aimed in my direction. "I had them made," he said. "Do you really like them?"

"Yes, Arthur. Of course I do. But—"

"Marry me, David. We've spent our lives together. The law accepts us now. Marry me. Please. Be my husband."

His face was solemn, his eyes eager. He sat so still waiting for my answer that I heard the leaves rustling in the branches of the hibiscus bushes just outside the kitchen window.

"Arthur—"

I lifted one of the rings from the box and slipped it over my finger. The golden bird sat perched on my hand, seemingly ready to fly off into the morning air. "It's a swallow," I said, studying the sheen of new gold on my finger. "Isn't it, Arthur? A swallow."

Arthur nodded. "A mission swallow. Remember how they swooped over our heads that day when we were sitting in the mission garden and we saw each other for the first time. Do you remember, David?"

"Of course, I remember. We were both so young. And about to tumble head over heels in love."

A smile touched Arthur's lips. "Yes."

I reached out for Arthur's hand, and pulling the second ring from the satin box, I slipped that ring over Arthur's finger. We both looked down at our two hands, adorned now with two mission swallows about to lift their golden bodies from the band of gold to soar off into the heavens.

"So *will* you, David? Will you marry me?"

I leaned across the breakfast table and took hold of Arthur's lapels to drag him toward me. We kissed with our faces hovering directly over a plate of toast.

He studied me as our lips slid apart. He was still waiting for an answer.

I reached up to push his hair back from his forehead. Grayer now, it still felt like cotton on my fingertips, just as it had four decades earlier when I first discovered its beauty.

"Of course I'll marry you, Arthur. Honestly, I had forgotten we weren't. We've been together so long, it just seems—*a given*—that we already are."

"Nothing is a given, David. Especially where love is concerned."

"Of course, you're right. I'm sorry."

Again I studied the rings on our fingers. I wasn't sure when it happened, but at some point Arthur's hand had found its way into mine. Having it there, I realized, also seemed a given.

Arthur lifted my hand and pressed it to his lips. He watched me with wide expectant eyes that peeked over the back of my hand. He was so excited there was a tremor in his touch. Or was the tremor mine? I couldn't tell.

"I love you, you know," he softly said.

"Yes, Arthur, I know. And I love you back."

Again, our eyes fell to the rings on our joined hands. And the beautiful golden swallows perched atop each one.

He glanced at his wristwatch. "I'm free today. How about you?"

"Just like that?" I asked. "Don't we have to arrange things first? Aren't there laws to obey? Protocols to follow? Witnesses to coerce? Cakes to order and invitations to be mailed?"

Arthur grinned as his lips once again grazed the back of my hand. "Done," he said. "I made an appointment for us at city hall. I had your best suit cleaned. I washed the gravy spot off your favorite tie. Fuck the cake—we're on a diet, as old people usually are, and the protocols can piss off. Witnesses are provided by the city for the modest fee of twenty bucks, which I happily shelled out in advance. All you have to do is comb your hair, wash your dick, get dressed, and tell me one more time you can't live without me."

I laughed, suddenly jubilant at doing what we would have undoubtedly done ages ago if the law had permitted. "I can't live without you, Arthur. And you know it too, don't you?"

He gave me a wink. "After forty years I was hoping."

He stood and tugged me toward him. "Let's go, David. Let's go now. I can't wait another decade."

I pushed my chair out of the way with a squeak and scooped him into my arms. "Yes," I said, burying my face in the side of his neck as I smiled at the way his hands instantly slid to my back, pulling me close. "Let's do it. Let's do it right this minute."

His lips laid themselves to my ear. "And later we'll have a date night."

"Date night, hell!" I roared, startling Sylvester, who dove off the fridge and took off running. "We'll have a *honeymoon* night! It'll be my best fantasy ever."

Arthur pushed me back to arm's length and studied my face. His eyes were soft with love, so worshipful and adoring they almost took my breath away.

"Thank you, David," he whispered, stroking my cheek. "Your best ever fantasy is all I've ever wanted to be."


IT WAS another hot day. Still the sun felt good on my face. Perhaps I was in a charitable mood because Arthur was walking at my side. It had been a while since we walked together. I had missed the camaraderie we shared sometimes even now, after all the years we'd spent in each other's company.

"How's your hip?" I asked. "Feeling better?"

"It'll do."

Something in his tone disturbed me. I stopped and stared at him. "What? What's wrong?"

He stopped when I did and turned back to study me. "You're going to love this."

"What?" I asked again. "*What* am I going to love?"

He pulled a handkerchief from his back pocket and blotted the sweat from his forehead, after removing his glasses first to get them out of the way. "I think I've run my last marathon. I'm simply too old to do another one."

I blinked at the weary acceptance in his eyes. My heart gave a sad little thud at the words he had used. "Why do you think that will make me happy?"

He shrugged. "You hate it when I run."

"No, I don't. I worry about you is all."

He aimed a lopsided smile in my direction. "You know that's not true, David. You hate me doing anything we don't do together."

I vehemently shook my head. "No. That's not true. I worry about you. That's all it is."

"You can say that as many times as you want, but you know it's still a lie."

I straightened my shoulders and slipped a hand through his arm. "Come on. Let's keep walking. There's no reason we can't walk and talk at the same time. And maybe you're right. Maybe I do hate it when we don't do things together."

Our footsteps echoed in the heat. The sun was directly above our heads, our shadows nonexistent. An older couple approached, walking a dog. I removed my arm from Arthur's. No sense flaunting our gayness in the face of every heterosexual we ran across. We have to live in the het world, after all. Or so I always told myself. Arthur, of course, didn't buy it for a minute. Never had.

He stubbornly looped his arm back through mine and laid our hands together so our two wedding rings would glisten in the sunlight. As we approached the couple, he tilted his head in greeting and with a huge smile, laid his head on my shoulder and sang out, "What a beautiful dog!"

The couple beamed with pride. "Thank you!" they sang back, nodding and raising their hands in greeting while their dog wagged his tail in appreciation as well. As they passed, the man gave us a final friendly wave, and the woman cried out, "Have a wonderful day, boys!"

When they were out of earshot, Arthur released my arm, lifted his head from my shoulder, and said, "See? We're just boys to them. You don't have to be afraid of what people think. Most people only see the good anyway. And since love is good, we have absolutely nothing to be ashamed of."

I groaned at his simplistic view of the world. The view he had carried in his heart since the day I met him. The view that probably made me fall in love with him to begin with. "*This* time, Arthur. You were right *this* time. Next time they might just as easily call us faggots and spit on our sneakers."

Arthur laughed. "In that case, fuck 'em, love. We'll just call them troglodytic breeders and spit right back."

I smiled. "You're too innocent for this world, Arthur."

He eyed me with a weary glower. "And you're too untrusting."

At that my smile widened. "I trust *you*."

Arthur stopped for a moment to flex his hip. It was bothering him again. I could see the pain of it in the set of his jaw. "That's because you know I would never do anything to hurt you."

"Yes," I said. "That's exactly why."

"I would never lie to you."

"No."

"I would never cheat on you."

"No, Arthur. You wouldn't."

"Not even in my imagination, David. Not even in the deepest darkest cellars of my mind. Not even there."

I dragged my gaze away from the earnest expression on his face, and shielding my eyes from the sun, I looked out to the purple horizon where the mountains of Mexico loomed in the distance.

"Let's get you home," I said. "You're stiffening up like an old loaf of bread."

Arthur grunted in agreement. "An apt analogy. And a slick way to change the subject."

"I'm not trying to change the subject."

"Yes, you are. You don't want to talk about your imaginary liaisons with every young male you run across."

I guffawed, or tried to. I must admit it sounded a little lame. Arthur was probably closer to the truth than even he knew. Actually, my flights of sexual fantasy were beginning to trouble even me. They were beginning to seem—a little too close to *real.*

"Arthur, we've been together almost forty years. Surely you know I love you."

"Do you ever imagine having sex with me, David? Or is that imaginary liaison too boring to contemplate?"

That I ignored. "Come along, Arthur. Let's get you home and put an ice pack on your hip."

"Heat," he groused.

"Ice," I said again.

And he flapped his hands in the air. "Oh, whatever, Dr. Oz."

We got a chuckle out of that because we both thought Dr. Oz was like the cutest medical practitioner *ever.* It was one of the few things we agreed on wholeheartedly.

We walked several blocks in companionable silence, our hands occasionally brushing as we traversed the familiar streets, careful where we stepped, as older people usually are.

I glanced down and saw that my shoelace was untied. Stopping, I bent to repair the problem as Arthur walked a few steps farther along. As I watched, I saw him stop in the middle of the block and gaze around at the surrounding houses. His head was cocked to the side, and as he turned to face me, I saw a look of confusion on his face. Confusion and maybe even a tiny trace of fear.

"What is it?" I asked. "What's wrong?"

Again, he studied the houses around us. He waited until I approached close enough that he could reach out his hand and touch my arm. His hand was shaking.

"Arthur, are you feeling ill? Is it the heat? What's wrong?"

He shook his head, the fear on his face was almost palpable. He stared at me with those bright azure eyes as he had never stared at me before. There was such need in his look. Such helplessness.

When he spoke, his voice was hushed. His words barely audible. He laid his hand on my forearm and his fingers clamped down tight, like tree roots seeking anchorage. "I don't know which way to go," he said. "I can't remember—"

My heart skipped a beat, but I forced myself to smile over it. "Can't remember what, love? What is it you can't remember?"

He drew in a great gulp of air as a lone tear skittered down his cheek.

"I can't remember where we live."

# Chapter Five

DR. WEI was pushing forty now. He had been our GP for ten years, and we trusted him implicitly. He was a small, handsome man of Chinese heritage with a kind manner and elegant little hands that brushed your skin like feathers when he wanted them to. At other times they could knead your flesh all the way down to the bone and make you shudder with ecstasy.

Let's just say Dr. Wei had a competent touch and leave it at that.

As long as we're discussing his good points, let me just say his voice was also kind. And at the moment, there happened to be a smile in it…

*"ARE YOU cold, David? What with your naked ass flapping in the wind and all, I thought you might be cold."*

*I forced up a chuckle but I had to work at it. I was, after all, in the doctor's examination room draped over the examining table on my stomach with the hospital gown untied behind me with my rear end, as the good doctor so cavalierly pointed out, on prominent display beneath the glare of what seemed to be one of those fucking searchlights used for movie premiers. Dr. Wei was sitting on a stool behind me, apparently having a good laugh at my expense.*

*The doctor gave my butt a couple of friendly pats which seemed to linger a little longer than was medically necessary. "You have a lovely ass, David. I'm sure Arthur tells you that all the time."*

*I broke out into one of those ecstatic shudders now. "Yes, he does," I managed to squeak. I felt a dribble of sweat roll down the side of my neck because my dick was lengthening beneath me, and I sincerely hoped the good doctor wasn't about to discover it creeping in his direction.*

*I heard the snap of latex, and a moment later the smell of lotion. After an expectant pause of perhaps three seconds, during which I did nothing but hold my breath in anticipation, I felt a gentle, lotion-coated fingertip, slide across my opening.*

*"Are you all right?" the doctor asked. I was almost certain he was still smiling. I was pretty sure it was a teasing one, too, if doctor's ever stoop to that sort of thing.*

*"I'm f-fine," I said, trying to control the tremor in my voice. With my weight pressing my hard-on into the paper sheet on the examination table, I was expending most of my willpower in the attempt to not start dry humping the table like a dog on his master's ankle.*

*"You'll feel a little pressure here," the doctor crooned as his finger slid into me like a tiny snake slithering down his hole. Before I could do so much as happily gasp, the doctor's hand was pressed against my ass and his finger was deep enough to give my prostate gland a delicious stroke of greeting.*

*I tensed, and the doctor laid his other hand atop my back as I felt his cheek rest against the side of my bare hip as he peered around to look at me.*

*"Am I hurting you?" he asked, his finger still buried in me as far as it would go.*

*"Not yet," I managed to gasp.*

*"Oh, good," the doctor said, and his finger began sliding in and out of my ass almost leisurely. Well, it was leisurely on his end. It was a little less than leisurely on mine. As a matter of fact, it was taking every ounce of willpower for me not to reach down and start stroking my cock.*

*Or better yet, maybe reaching around to stroke the doc's.*

*"A little more pressure," the doctor cooed as a second finger worked its way into me beside the first. "And just a wee manipulation to stimulate the prostate."*

*His two fingers lovingly brushed my prostate, and I squeezed my eyes shut in bliss and opened my legs a little* wider to give the doctor easier access. Not that he wasn't accessed up to the hilt already.

As my legs spread wider, the doctor said, "I see your balls now, David. Perhaps I should examine them while I'm at it. You never know when lumps may form. Testicular cancer is a very real risk for men of your age. This won't hurt at all." He finished speaking at the same time the cool fingers of his free hand, this one unsheathed in latex, slid beneath my ball sac and tested the weight of my testicles. Simultaneously, the two fingers he had burrowed deep inside me gave another friendly scrape across my prostate.

"Holy hell," I muttered, pressing my face into the examination table and spreading my legs even wider.

"I seem to have hit a nerve," the doctor said behind me. This time when he spoke, I could feel his breath brushing softly across my ass, and what do you know, my legs spread even more.

"No pain?" he asked softly.

"Are you kidding?" I said around a mouthful of paper sheeting. My dick was now so hard I could feel a dribble of precome dampening my own belly button.

"Let's try one more, shall we?" Dr. Wei asked as if he was considering a third cup of coffee. And before I knew what he was about to do, I felt a third finger slide into me alongside the other two.

With my arms splayed out over my head and dangling off the other side of the examining table, I turned my head to the side and bit down on my bicep just to keep myself from screaming in rapture.

With three fingers buried in me and sliding in and out in tandem, with every single stroke adding another explosion of heaven to my quivering prostate, and with the doc's free hand now cupping my balls and his fingers pressed along the underside of my cock (when had that happened?), it was all I could do not to come right then and there.

"You seem tense," the doctor said. "Are you sure I'm not hurting you?"

*This time when he spoke I felt the brush of his lips on the inside of my thigh. Before I could come to grips with that sensation, his free hand squeezed a path further beneath me until his fingers circled my cock completely.*

*"Well, then, what have we here?" he asked. And as his fingers circled the head of my dick and my ass rose up in the air to accommodate it, still packed as it was with three of the good doctor's fingers, I might add, I gave a great shuddering gasp and filled the doctor's hand with come. As the juices surged out of me, he continued to stroke and prod my jewel deep inside. And when the last splash of semen exited my cock and dribbled across his hand, the doctor rested his face to the back of my leg, just below where the thigh meets the ass, and there he planted a gentle kiss.*

*"Thank you, David," the doctor said, pulling his face from me, releasing my cock, and giving my still-trembling ass a friendly caress with his come-soaked hand.*

*"Thank you," I managed to sputter.*

*And before the doctor pulled his fingers free of my all-too-hungry ass, he gave my prostate a final nudge as if to say good-bye.*

*I met his nudge with a final shudder of my own.*

*A moment later the doctor's fingers slid free, leaving me as empty as I had ever felt in my life. With a last squeeze of my drained cock, that hand, too, slipped away from me. Behind me I once again heard the snap of latex when the doctor pulled off his glove.*

*"Now then," he said. "Let's check that blood pressure."*

IT WAS a year from the day Arthur proposed to me at the breakfast table. A year from the day we strolled into the San Diego County Courthouse single gay men and departed a married couple. On this day, exactly one year later, we stood in a doctor's office not a block and a half from that courthouse, this time with another monumental event reshaping our lives.

Arthur was waiting in the hall, just outside the doctor's door. I could hear him softly humming to himself. Dr. Wei, a dear friend as well as our physician, poked a few keys on his computer, then stopped and cocked his head toward the sound. A tiny smile lit his face.

"Arthur's on key," he said.

I smiled back. "He always is."

The doctor nodded as if he expected as much. "It's dementia, David. I guess you knew that." His voice was soft. He obviously didn't want Arthur to overhear.

It was my turn to nod. Of the three of us, the only one still smiling now was Arthur. I could hear the smile in his gentle hum through the doctor's closed door.

"I suspected. But—"

"Yes?"

"He's just so young! Sixty-one. I thought dementia patients were, you know, *old.*"

The doctor laughed. "David, it may come as a surprise to you, but some people consider sixty one to *be* old. But you're right, of course. Arthur is young for this diagnosis. Still, it happens. When the patient is diagnosed with dementia under the age of sixty-five, the disease is considered early onset dementia. Rita Hayworth acquired it in her fifties, although they thought it was simply the effects of alcoholism at the time. Her problem was eventually diagnosed as full-blown Alzheimer's, of course. But still, you get the idea. It's not that uncommon, David. Not at Arthur's age."

I straightened the crease of my pant leg, just to have something to do. I noticed my hands were shaking as I did. "But it happened so fast, Doc. I noticed little things happening now and then, taking his shoes and socks off after church, forgetting to pay the bills, losing his train of thought, but then yesterday, suddenly, he no longer remembered where we live. How could it happen so quickly?"

The doctor crossed his legs and folded his hands together on his knee, swiveling his chair as he did it to study me. "The disease has probably been building for quite a while. If we aren't looking for the symptoms of dementia in a loved one, they can slip past us quite easily until the dementia manifests itself completely. Don't look so glum, David. In a way you are lucky."

I couldn't believe what I was hearing. "How can you say that?"

He unclasped his hands and reached out to pat my knee. "David, I have no doubt that Arthur will still be with you for many years to come. He may need a little extra care and a bit more watching to keep him out of harm's way, but he will still be Arthur for a very long time. It isn't Alzheimer's, David. It's simple dementia. Trust me, you're lucky. Both of you are. It's not a walk in the park, but on the other hand, David, it won't kill him. Alzheimer's would."

"What should I do? Should I tell him? Does he know?"

He lifted his hand from my knee and fiddled with a pencil on his desk, tapping out a little rhythm to the tune of Arthur's song. I realized Arthur was humming the "Jet Song" from *West Side Story*.

"David, if you are asking if I told him the diagnosis, the answer is no. Not yet. I wanted to talk to you about it first. If you're asking for my opinion, I would have to say yes. We should tell him. Sometimes not knowing what is wrong can do more harm to the patient than knowing. Stress levels go up. Fear kicks in. And in the long run, what good would it accomplish, not telling him? " He leaned forward and tapped the pencil on my knee. "What I'm saying is, he will understand. He knows something is wrong already, and we should tell him now while he is still capable of grasping the truth of it all. The fear of not knowing would be infinitely worse for him, David. I truly believe that."

I gazed down at my hands and saw they were still shaking. *Well, why the hell wouldn't they be?*

"He's going to forget me, isn't he, Doctor? He's going to forget he loves me."

"No!" the doctor barked, once again taking my hand, this time rolling his chair a little closer to mine so he could reach out and pat my cheek. "Don't be silly, David. He's not going to forget he loves you. Dementia patients are ordinarily able to remember their loved ones, many even toward the very end of their lives. Their judgment will be impaired, but their hearts are not. With Alzheimer's it's a different story." His face split into a grin. "He talked about you all the time I was testing him, you know. Telling me what a wonderful person you are. Telling me about the day you married."

My heart tumbled in my chest. "So he hasn't forgotten that."

"No. Of course not. And he probably never will. David, he's at the very beginning of the disease. There will be days, even weeks, maybe months, when you notice nothing at all out of sync. He is still living the life he's always lived. He's still the same man he always was."

I sucked in a deep breath and tried to steady myself as the doctor pulled his hand away and repositioned himself in a more doctorly manner on his little rolling chair.

"So what should we do, then, Doctor? Nothing?" I tried to bite back the sarcasm in my voice, but I'm not sure I succeeded very well.

"Like I said, he is still in the beginning phases. I'll bet if you went back to the place where he told you he forgot where he lived, he would remember the way home now. These memories, or I should say these *gaps* in memory, will come and go. At least for a time. And Arthur is a healthy man otherwise. I suspect he will weather this storm for quite a while before it really puts a damper on his activities. You want my advice? Take a trip. Take a trip now while he still has most of his faculties. Reconnect with each other, not that you don't seem pretty connected already. Make him happy. Make him smile. Show him how much you love him."

I couldn't decide if what he was suggesting was the dumbest thing I'd ever heard or the most brilliant. "But where would we go? Where should I take him?"

Dr. Wei thought about that for a moment, all the while still tapping his pencil to the tune of Arthur's humming out in the hall, which I realized now had gone from the "Jet Song" to

"I Feel Pretty." Arthur always did love *West Side Story*. I had to smile listening to him.

"Arthur will experience moments of fear and confusion as he senses his mind slipping away on occasion. To overpower that fear, you need to make him know how loved he is."

This time when my heart tumbled in my chest, it tumbled from guilt. I hadn't exactly been a paragon of competence when it came to making Arthur feel loved lately.

"I hope he knows that already" I heard myself say. But did he really? I wondered.

Dr. Wei's eyes brightened. "Take him to where you first met. It was somewhere up the coast, wasn't it? I seem to recall Arthur telling me that during one visit or other."

"Yes," I said. "We met in San Juan Capistrano. At the mission."

He smiled broadly and snapped his fingers, giving me a glimpse of the actual man beneath the doctor's persona. The *kind* man. The man I had always found so appealing. "That's right! He told me that once. He told me you met in the garden of the old mission. He was sitting on a bench and you came up to talk to him. He said he had known he could love you before you even opened your mouth to speak."

Again I found myself blinking back tears. "He actually said that? To you?"

"Yes, David, he did. I have a feeling Arthur has a very romantic soul."

"He does indeed."

"Recommit yourself to him, David. Take him to the mission. Spur his memory to remember the days of your past. Let him know he's still loved, just as much as he still loves you. It will do him good. It might even do you both good."

I patted my chest to still my thumping heart. "You're a smart man," I said, rising from the chair.

He stood to face me. "And I've been your doctor for a very long time. May I give you a hug?"

"Y-yes."

He felt cool and crisp as he stepped into my arms. As his small hands patted my back, he whispered softly into my ear. "Think of it as a second honeymoon, David. Do it. Make Arthur happy. I'll even babysit your goddamn cat for you while you're gone."

That made me laugh in earnest. "Sylvester? Sorry, Doc, but now I'm afraid you've bitten off more than you can fucking chew."


IT'S ODD how quickly the years of a lifetime speed by. You blink your eyes and discover they have clicked past, one by one by one, like the tumbling pages of a Rolodex, moving so fast they become nothing but a blur of shadows and light and faint, faint echoes of sound.

The individual moments of that lifetime, both the real and the imaginary, fly by even faster, until there are only flashes of a select few memories left to study in those idle moments when you find yourself wondering where it all went.

Looking back on my life now, somehow it's the imaginary moments that bother me most. Why did I waste my time on them? Why did I let them take control of my life? It wasn't from loneliness or for a lack of love that I turned to erotic fantasies. I have no need for illusions when I have Arthur there beside me every step of the way, knowing now, as I did then, that no one could love me more than he. Nor could I have more completely loved anyone in return.

Arthur has always been the one real constant in my long journey toward growing old. He has been the only unstinting truth I have found along the way, my love for him the only unchanging emotion that has filled my heart from the day we declared ourselves to each other. Loving him, and being loved *by* him, is my one great accomplishment in life.

The men in my imaginary trysts were empty shadows. Arthur was flesh and blood and generosity and honor. He has never once called his feelings for me anything other than what they are. He has never once turned his eyes to another man when I was there beside him. He has never once made me feel ashamed that I was perhaps not everything he needed, everything he hungered for.

Arthur has taught me what it is to be loved. Unconditionally. Completely.

And while I have loved him back—*I have*—I have not loved him back with the commitment he deserves.

I did not realize this fact until the day he stared at me with those frightened eyes and declared himself lost—*lost not three blocks from our home*.

It was then, at that precise moment on our long journey together, that I finally understood our days together were numbered. They were not infinite at all, as I had always led myself to believe.

I think Arthur realized it for the first time that day too.

"I can't remember where we live," he had said. With the burn of rising tears in my eyes, I pulled him into my arms to hide them from his view.

It was there, as I look back on that moment, on that red-hot sidewalk in front of a stranger's house not three blocks from the home we had shared for forty years, that I said good-bye to Arthur for the very first time, just as he had admitted his leaving to me. Not in so many words maybe. But the truth was suddenly there before us, and we both knew it.

I squeezed my eyes shut against the image of Mr. B and Mr. C snuggled unmoving on that four-poster bed with the canopy above their heads that matched the quilt beneath their bodies. When I opened my eyes to the sun and the breeze and the scent of oleander growing along the street, but most importantly to Arthur still standing there before me in terror, a terror he had perhaps never seen coming at all, I swore then and there I would make the rest of his journey safe. I would make the rest of his journey happy.

Just as he had always made my own.

"PACK YOUR bags, Arthur. We're taking a trip."

The house smelled delicious because Arthur was at that very moment pulling a meat loaf out of the oven. Arthur's meat loaves are legendary. At least in my mind. The fact that it was nowhere near dinnertime didn't seem to bother Arthur any more than it bothered me. Nor did it bother him that I had told him I would pick up dinner on my way home, which explained the sack of fried chicken under my arm. I simply tucked the bag into the fridge before he noticed. While I was on that side of the kitchen, I turned off the oven, which he also seemed to have forgotten.

Meat loaf poised in midair, Arthur blinked back the steam and asked, "Where are we going?" If he noticed anything I had been doing, it didn't register on his face.

So I simply gave him my brightest smile, and said, "Memory lane."

"Where's that?" he asked, carefully placing the bubbling Pyrex pan on the kitchen counter.

"It's in our past. You'll remember it when you see it."

He looked doubtful. "Will I? I seem to be having a hard time remembering *any*thing lately. Sometimes I don't even feel like me anymore. Fucking dementia."

My heart gave a tiny lurch of anguish. "You're still you, my love. You'll always be you. Who the hell else would you be?"

"Oh. Well, then, I guess it's okay." He made a few slices through the meat loaf with a steak knife and more steam billowed out, fogging up the kitchen window. My saliva glands produced about a quart of spit and tried to drown me with it.

He smiled sweetly, as if his doubts of five seconds earlier had dissipated already. "Unless we're leaving right this minute on this little trip to round up ancient memories, how about sour cream on your baked potato? I seem to remember that much about what you like."

I walked up to him and pulled the knife from his hand to lay it aside. As soon as he was unarmed, I pulled him into an embrace and buried my face in the crook of his neck. He smelled of onion and minced garlic. He seemed surprised by my attentions, but in less than three second flat, his face was buried in *my* neck. One thing about Arthur, he's always ready to reciprocate love at a moment's notice. Even with dinner steaming on the table.

His hands were on my back as he said, "What's gotten into you?"

I shrugged in his arms. "Just a girl in love, I guess."

He pushed me to arm's length and eyed me with good-natured suspicion. "Okay, David. What are you up to? I know you love me, but as you damn well know, you're usually about as demonstrative as a bucket of gravel. It's also time for your near-naked jogger to go clomping by. Shouldn't you be at the living room window playing with yourself and coming on the drapery?"

I smiled under his teasing, which was actually rather strange since any other time his comment about my favorite jogger might have pissed me off. "Crass," I said. "I like that."

He blinked in surprise. "You *do*?"

I thought perhaps a gentle lie was in order. "When I'm fantasizing about that jogger, I'm really thinking about you. You do know that, don't you?"

"N-no. I didn't know that at all."

My hand slipped down his back and a few adventurous fingers wormed their way beneath his waistband. The swell of his ass felt warm and inviting as only familiar terrain can feel. I watched Arthur tilt his head back and close his eyes when one particularly brave finger dove into the crack of his ass and began reconnoitering the immediate vicinity.

Eyes still closed, he breathed, "Aren't you hungry?"

"Yes," I said. "Starving." And to prove it I pulled him tighter against me and laid my mouth over his, sucking in his lower lip and nipping at it softly with my teeth. The gambit seemed to be paying off. I could tell by the suddenly substantial bulge pressing against my hip, which, if I knew my way around the male anatomy, and I did, I was pretty sure was Arthur's blood-glutted pecker doing an eager reconnaissance of its own.

I still had Arthur's bottom lip sucked into my mouth like a Popsicle, so when he spoke, his diction wasn't exactly top-notch. "Do thixty-five-year-old queenth have thex in the middle of the day while there'th a perfectly good meat loaf thitting on the table waiting to be conthumed?"

"Shut up, Arthur," I said. And he did. Not only did he shut up, he also wiggled his ass around to make a little extra room for my invading finger. I told you he was accommodating.

I released his lip and buried the fingers of my free hand in his hair. Taking a gentle fistful of it, I eased his head to the side, then pressed my lips against his ear. When I whispered my words, I heard the sexy huskiness in my voice. Arthur wilted a little bit in my grasp. He must have heard it too.

"I want to make love to you," I breathed into him. "Right now."

He simply nodded and began tugging my shirttail out of my slacks. While he did that, he kicked off his shoes. My marauding finger, which was still buried in the seat of his pants, had by this time found the silken flesh of his opening, hot and moist with perspiration. When I scraped a fingertip across it, Arthur shuddered in my arms.

"Aren't we a little old to be—"

"Shut up," I said again. And once again he clammed up. This time he was smiling when he did it.

"Can I fuck you?" I asked.

His lips found the hollow at the base of my throat. I felt his tongue taste my flesh there. My dick was beginning to ache in the confinement of my trousers and underwear.

Again, Arthur nodded against me. "Yes," he said. "I'm ready. I always try to be ready."

"I know you do, baby."

He was wearing a T-shirt, so I simply tugged it over his head and out of the way. His pale torso was still beautiful. And somehow the fact that I knew every inch of the man made it even more beautiful. When I sucked his nipple into my mouth, he groaned. He drew in a truckload of air and trembled when I slid my tongue across his tit. His fingers were in my hair now. He held me against him like a mother offering sustenance to an infant.

"Oh God, David. Your mouth feels so good."

I smiled, wondering at myself. How many times had I missed the opportunity to do exactly this over the past forty years? How many times had I let Arthur go untouched? Unexplored. Unpleased. How many times had I simply walked away from the man and headed into one of my fantasies when he was always here, ready for me. Always ready. And all I had to do was ask.

"I love you so much," I muttered against his skin, and easing myself to my knees, I dragged my lips down his stomach until his belly button was there in front of me. The scattering of reddish hair around it tickled my nose. The heated scent of him once again all but took my breath away. Even now, forty years after we met on that stone bench in the mission garden up the coast, there wasn't an ounce of fat on Arthur. He was as beautiful as the first day I held him.

Even more beautiful, perhaps. For what is more beautiful that knowing exactly what you have before you? What is more beautiful than caressing a man who you know—*you just know*—has never for an entire lifetime loved anyone but you?

My hands were shaking as I unclasped Arthur's belt buckle and popped the button at the top of his jeans. I slid his zipper slowly down, exposing a spray of pale pubic hair and the base of his fat cock, just peeking through the opening. *No underwear. That's my boy.*

With his fingers still buried in my hair, he looked down at me as I tugged his jeans down to his knees and freed his cock from its denim prison. The moment it saw the light of day and felt the clean air of freedom, it boinged into the atmosphere and whapped me in the face, causing both of us to laugh.

I ignored his cock for the moment as one by one I cradled his feet and lifted them from the floor, tugging his pant legs over them. In moments, he was standing before me completely naked. I squatted on my haunches at his feet and looked up over the clean lines of his long, pale body, and as I stared at him, I pulled my own clothes away and flung them across the kitchen.

He gazed down at me with the sexiest smile I had ever seen on a human face. His fingers took a gentle hold of his erect cock and eased his foreskin away from his glans, exposing it to me completely. With his other hand still buried in my hair, he pulled my face toward him until my cheek and his dick were huddled next to each other.

The heat of him was astounding. I kissed the base of his cock and, at the same time, gripped my own dick in my fist and gave it a couple of pumps, assuring myself I was ready. Needless to say, I most certainly was.

I slipped his cock into my mouth and tasted the moisture coating the tip of it, a taste I knew perfectly. It was a nectar I never tired of sipping.

When he was shaking like crazy and the backs of his knees were all but knocking against the kitchen counter behind him, I let him pull me to my feet. With one more kiss on the lips, just because I couldn't seem to allow myself to leave them untouched, I took Arthur's hand and led him across the kitchen to the breakfast table.

"Oh God," he muttered as I eased him around to place his back to my front and slowly pressed his torso down to the tabletop, exposing his ass to me completely.

I could barely understand what he was saying when he pointed to the cupboard behind me. "Oil, butter, Crisco," he gasped. "Anything."

I bent and slid a tongue between the splayed mounds of his ass, and he erupted into a new burst of trembling. Then I reached out to tug open the cabinet door and plucked the first bottle I saw off the shelf.

I stared at the label, most of my thinking centered on my dick, not on what I held in my hand. "Balsamic vinegar okay?"

"Uh, no," Arthur moaned, lifting his ass and begging me to enter him *now*. "I don't think so, dumbass. Grab something else."

I set the vinegar bottle aside and grabbed a bottle of Wesson oil off the shelf. It was a new bottle, never before opened. I cranked the lid off and tossed it in the sink behind me, which startled the cat and sent him flying into the other room with a hiss. Turning back to Arthur, I bent to kiss the small of his back and his hand reached around behind him and stroked my cheek when I did.

Filling the palm of my hand with oil, I pressed it to his ass and lubricated him thoroughly. With his body heat warming the oil, I eased a finger inside him to assure myself he was properly lubricated, and when he muttered "yes" with his mouth smashed against the tabletop, I knew we were good to go.

I coated my cock with the remaining oil on my hand, and as I pushed it against his opening, I leaned over him and whispered into his ear, "Are you ready?"

He nodded as if words were beyond his ability to speak. Stretching his arms out in front of him, he grasped the opposite edge of the table to brace himself, and I gently leaned over him. On tiptoe, I pushed myself harder into him as Arthur opened himself up to me. I watched in wonder as my cock slid ever deeper into that warm, delicious ass that I had pierced so many times before. When Arthur was impaled upon me completely and shuddering and bucking beneath me, I leaned over him once again and pressed my lips to the back of his neck as I began to move.

"Oh yes," we muttered in unison, breathless. "Oh, David, yes," Arthur said.

As we lost ourselves to the tactile sensation of flesh entering flesh, of hunger meeting hunger, our love seemed to hang around us like the scent of Arthur's meat loaf, permeating the room. Permeating ourselves.

It was then, at that precise moment, that I understood for the very first time even a lifetime of love was not enough.

Not for Arthur. Not for me.

We needed more.

OUR ANNIVERSARY cake was huge. Far bigger than eight friends, two lovers, and a couple of parents required. There was a huge number 10, rendered in inedible blue plastic, stabbed into the frosting along with ten varicolored candles. The ten candles were lit with orange flames, and Arthur cradled the cake with both hands as he made a grand entrance through the kitchen door with the damn thing to join everyone in the dining room. I was trailing along behind him with two gallon buckets of ice cream. One vanilla, one rocky road.

Our eight friends clapped and carried on as good friends usually do on occasions such as this, but Arthur's parents were hard-pressed to dredge up so much as a smile. They were in town on business, not for our anniversary, and later they twice cornered me in one room or the other to tell me so, but only after consuming a goodly portion of the fucking cake.

After the third such whispered announcement, I walked away (it was his mother delivering the declaration that time), and as far as I can remember, it is the last time we exchanged words at all. And I mean *ever.*

I have to give Arthur credit. He understood my feelings perfectly. Not only did he understand them, but he laid down an ultimatum to his mother and father later that very evening after the other guests had gone and we were cleaning up the mess from our little anniversary shindig.

The ultimatum from their son was this: *accept my lover or get the fuck out of our house.*

Their response was immediate and permanent. They got the fuck out and never returned, hopping a flight the very next day to their country estate in Penzance, situated safely across the pond from the perverted faggot their son had taken up with.

They shunned not only me, but also Arthur, their only son. And they did it through all the remaining years of their lives, which were numerous.

But we wouldn't learn about that until later.

After the party, with our guests safely ushered out the door and the house once again to ourselves, Arthur helped me clean up the mess. He stood wiping dishes and stacking them in the cupboard while I finished washing the silverware. Occasionally he would bump me with his hip to make me smile.

"Don't feel bad," he said, bumping me again. "If they can't see how lucky they are to have you as a son-in-law, they don't deserve to be part of our circle. They always were a pair of bloody standoffish twits. How they were lucky enough to produce a clever chap such as me for a son, I'll never know. Maybe Mum bonked the postman while Pop was out playing cricket. He used to, you know. Used to go on and on over dinner about grubbers and googlies and nurdling."

Suds went everywhere when Arthur scooped me into his arms, yanking my hands out of the dishwater to do it. A fork and two knives clattered to the floor. Stacy, our pet beagle at the time, yelped and dove under the kitchen table in case more WMDs came cascading in her direction.

Somehow, Arthur's reassurance made me feel worse. "I shouldn't have walked away from her. I should have just nodded and bowed and complimented her dress or something."

Arthur gave me a good-natured grunt. "They would have found another reason to leave. They've been itching to ever since they got here."

"Have they?"

"Yes, love, but not because of you. I guess Dad wanted another chucker in the family. But not only did I end up not playing cricket, I left the bloody continent altogether and married a Yank. A *male* Yank."

"We aren't married," I said.

"No, and I don't suppose we ever will be. Not legally. But in our hearts we are. And if my family can't accept that fact, then fuck 'em." He tossed the dishtowel onto the counter and placed his two hands on either side of my face as his azure eyes studied me from a distance of about six inches. "You do feel married, don't you?"

I smiled. "You're fishing."

"Let me try again," he said. "You do feel married, don't you?"

I chuckled and placed my hands in the exact same position on his face as he was holding mine.

"Yes, Arthur. I feel married. I love you more than anything. We may not be connected by law, but we are most certainly connected by heart and a shitload of legal documents. If you should die on me, I'm not about to let them waltz in here and take everything, you know."

He grinned. "That was my idea."

"And a damned good one."

He took a deep breath, and his mouth turned up in a lazy smile. "What do Yanks do on their tenth anniversaries? In England, I understand they have it off. Maybe we could try that."

I laughed. "If having it off means a spirited roll in the hay, I'm all for it."

Arthur grimaced. "A roll in the hay. Sounds rather itchy. Fancy a fuck in the bed, instead?"

I grinned. "That would be lovely, ducks."

And lovely it was.


AFTER ALL the years since that tenth anniversary party, Arthur's reaction to his parents' snub still amazed me.

"You never looked back," I said. "And you never left the States again."

Arthur gave a tiny shrug but never pulled his eyes from the grand Pacific Ocean sliding past on our left. His mind was apparently elsewhere than where I had been trying to steer it by rattling on about his parents for the last few minutes.

"Isn't technology wonderful?" he asked. "I remember when we first rode this train forty years ago. It was like riding a log wagon with square wheels. Bumpy and jerky and noisy as hell. Now it's more like flight than rail travel, only without all the TSA bullshit. This train is whisper silent and as smooth as silk. It's all I can do to stay awake, David." Belying the truth of that statement, he pointed to a sign slipping past outside the window, as excited as a six-year-old on his first roller coaster. "Del Mar is coming up!"

He unfolded his hands from his lap. One of them he used to pull the curtain closed to block out the view, and the other he laid over mine on the armrest between us. "Sorry. You were saying?" he asked. "Something about Mum, wasn't it?"

"Yes," I said. "Your folks. You turned your back on them. And you did it for the love of me."

His thumb massaged my wrist. "I didn't turn my back on them. They turned their backs on us. There's a difference. What was that line from *Dirty Dancing*? 'Nobody puts baby in the corner'? Well, you're my baby. And I damn well let them know it."

He watched a man and his two young daughters scurrying down the aisle with armloads of chow from the snack car. The man was handsome and tall, and before I knew what I was doing, an imaginary tryst was beginning to take shape in my head. I quickly and guiltily snipped it away like a surgeon excising a piece of diseased flesh.

As the man and his two daughters disappeared into seats several rows in front of us, Arthur added, "And I didn't turn my back on them completely. I rang them up a few times over the years. We kept in touch."

"You never told me that."

"No. I didn't."

I thought about what he had just said, and as I did so, I felt a weight lift from my chest.

"I'm glad," I said. "I'm glad you kept in touch. I hated they had lost you. I hated that I was the one who made it happen. They were really lovely people."

He cackled like a startled rooster. "Oh please! And you didn't make anything happen. *They* did."

I felt a grin creep across my face. "So did they ever ask about me? You know, over the years when you were ringing them up. Did they ever ask how I was?"

Arthur giggled. "Uh. No. Nary a peep. According to them, one might think you never existed at all."

We shared a glance, and the next thing I knew we were howling with laughter. When I managed to get control of myself, I said, "At least they didn't hold a grudge. They still left you all their money when they died."

"Yes, but not the property in Penzance. That they left to the London Zoo. A last kick in the butt, I guess. Asserting their authority."

Our gaze met like two reluctant strangers, and the next thing I knew we were howling with laughter *again*.

"The bastards," he sputtered, stomping his feet in glee like a kid. "Do you suppose there are rhinos and emus having tea in the old parlor with my mother's good china? Was my room taken over by mole rats? Do they have a flock of mountain goats keeping the verge trimmed and a fucking family of giraffes cropping the yew trees in the back yard so the branches don't bang against the upstairs windows in the winter, keeping everybody awake?"

I wiped happy tears from my face and clutched Arthur's hand all the tighter. "I wonder if they ever hung a portrait of me over the mantel."

"Probably not," he said, every tooth in his head exposed in one of those smiles that always made my heart do a backflip it was just so damn beautiful. "Although they undoubtedly would not have been averse to hanging *you* over the goddamn mantel."

After a few minutes, we got control of ourselves, and as Arthur opened the drapes to once again take in the view of the California coast gliding past, I reached under my seat and hauled out a paper bag. I lowered the serving trays in front of us and began emptying the bag.

"Lunch," I explained, as I passed out foil-wrapped fried chicken from the lot I had brought home the day before, and also meat loaf sandwiches left over from the dinner Arthur had prepared because he had forgotten I was bringing home chicken. I excused myself and toddled off to the snack car for sodas and was back in minutes, doling them out with ice and straws and pretty little Amtrak napkins to keep things civilized.

Without further ado, we tucked into lunch, consuming everything I had laid out.

After the feeding frenzy was over, we settled back into our seats and watched the surfers out on the water with their longboards and their wetsuits.

"Look how lovely they are," Arthur sighed. "So young and lithe and trim." He turned worried eyes to me. "Do you miss our youth, David? Do you miss the effortless ease with which we did things when we were in our twenties? Do you miss the way we carried ourselves and how nothing ever hurt and how the world was one great continual moment of discovery?"

I turned the question back on him. "No. Do you?"

He turned to face me. Not quite shy. Not quite fearless. When he shook his head, he did it with such assurance I once again felt my heart stutter inside my chest. "No. It's still the same world for me, David. As long as you're with me, it always will be."

"Ditto," I smiled.

He threw a fake grump in my direction. "Such a romantic word. Ditto. You have the heart of a poet. Asshole."

I laughed, and soon he was laughing with me.

We stared out through the window at the world slipping past. With his hand still snuggled into mine and the gentle swaying of the railroad car around us, I thought back to my visit with Dr. Wei. The things we had discussed seemed so silly now. I wasn't losing Arthur. His mind wasn't about to fly off a fucking trestle somewhere up ahead on life's railroad tracks. He was still the same man I had lived with for forty years. The same man I had married a year before. The same man I had only recently learned to appreciate again.

As the train swept around a bend in the tracks, leaving the ocean behind and diving into a sea of cookie-cutter condos amid a forest of blooming jacaranda trees, Arthur turned his gentle eyes to me and smiled a blushing smile.

"I've forgotten," he said. "Where the hell are we going?"

And at that moment, a sign reading San Juan Capistrano skidded past the window.

Arthur blinked when he saw it.

"Ah," he said, his eyes lighting up and a soft smile twisting his lips. His hand took a firmer grip on mine as he leaned into me and whispered, "Now I remember."

WHILE WE waited to detrain, I thought back to our twentieth anniversary. No simple dinner party marked the occasion. Bigger ceremonies had been planned.

I remembered every moment of the day. Every single moment.

A mixed bag of humanity stood in a throng before the War Memorial Building in Balboa Park, a stone's throw from the gates of the San Diego Zoo. The faces in that throng were as varied as the faces of humanity itself. Old, young, Asian, Hispanic, white, black, feeble, hale. In the center of the crowd, a face I had not taken my eyes from since he stepped away from me and took up his place with the others.

Arthur was decked out in his best suit. He wore an outrageous tie he had purchased for the occasion. The tie was blue and red and splashed with white stars. He stood beneath the blazing hot sun looking as handsome as ever, his strawberry hair ablaze in the light, his shoulders broad, his back straight. In his forties now, Arthur was every bit as stunning as he had been when I first spotted him on that stone bench in the mission garden at Capistrano on the day that began our long journey together. There was a proud glint in his eye as he stared out across the crowd to find me standing where he had left me on the lawn at the base of the flagpole. Old Glory hung limp in the windless midday heat above my head.

Arthur wore a wondrous expression on his face that day, not unlike a child on Christmas morning. We had talked about this for years, of course, but only recently had Arthur decided to stop talking and do something about it.

At the sound of static blasting through the loudspeakers somewhere on the walls of the War Memorial, all heads, including mine, turned toward the flag above my head. The first notes of the National Anthem were tinny and scratchy—the recording must have been decades old—but by the time the first bridge was reached, I didn't notice the poor sound quality any more. I was too busy swallowing the lump of pride that kept threatening to choke me.

Standing with respect, my hand over my heart, I stared out across the heads of the crowd and saw Arthur standing next to an old Chinese woman who must have been ninety and was so short she barely came up to Arthur's breastbone. Arthur had one hand over his heart, as I and everyone else did, and his other hand had gripped the old woman's elbow to steady her. Grateful, perhaps, for his assistance, she had leaned toward him as if they were old friends. I wondered vaguely if I was the only one in the crowd who knew they had not met more than a minute earlier. Even from a distance, I could see tears streaming down both their cheeks. Just as tears were streaming down mine.

As the final beats of the anthem faded to silence, all heads slowly turned to the podium at the top of the steps leading into the memorial. There a man had taken his place before a microphone. To either side of him stood the American and California flags. They hung unfurled but still in the windless noonday air.

My gaze remained glued to Arthur's back as he stared up to the podium with his hand still on the old Chinese woman's elbow. He stood straight and proud, as did the other sixty or seventy people around him.

I fished in my back pocket for a handkerchief and blew my nose. Quietly. I was happy to hear a few other sniffs among the witnesses gathered around me, watching their own loved ones declare loyalty to their new homeland.

When the oath was taken, the sonorous murmur of all those voices speaking in unison unleashed the tears from my eyes, just as they did many others. Later, after the oath was completed and the proclamations of citizenship made, a moment of silence reigned over the crowd as the man at the podium turned and walked away. At that moment the first gust of morning wind stirred the flags atop the memorial steps, and when it did, Arthur turned his eyes to me and waved.

As the group of new American citizens wended their way toward their loved ones and those who were there that day to share the moment with them, I watched as Arthur stooped and kissed the cheek of the old woman beside him. When she smiled and reached up with her withered hand to brush the tears from Arthur's cheek, I felt my own tears spill across my lashes.

Arthur spoke a final word to the woman, and turning from her, he made his way across the grass to me.

Speechless, I watched him approach—tall, lean, proud. When we stood toe to toe, he patted his chest as if still trying to calm the pounding of his heart.

"I'm American now," he softly said.

And without another word, he took my arm and led me toward the car.


THEN I thought of another trip and another anniversary. Our twenty-fifth.

And the first and last time I ever *truly* cheated on the man I loved.

The cabin lay sprawled beneath a stand of conifers that blocked the view of Half Dome Mountain in the distance, unless you walked out onto the road to see it, which Arthur and I had just done.

As we stood there on the macadam roadway, staring around us at the rocky cliffs and majestic beauty of a gazillion acres of pristine forestland, Arthur took my hand and sighed deeply. "It won't be the same without you."

I chucked him on the arm. "Don't be silly. You'll be with a group. The permit is already paid for. Go and have fun. I'm just going to lounge around the cabin, and by this evening, I'll be back to normal. I'll take you up to the lodge for dinner when you get back. My headache should be better by then."

He shuffled his feet. "Well—"

I chucked him again. "Just watch whar yer goin' and don't git et up by a bear."

He giggled. "Okay, Daniel Boone."

"And don't fall off any cliffs."

He rolled his eyes. "I won't, Mommy."

"And don't be fucking around with any fellow hikers. It's a nature hike, not a wilderness fuckfest."

Arthur tilted his head to the side and gave me one of his "patient" looks. Living with me for twenty-five years, he had managed to pretty well perfect that look by now. Apparently I required a lot of patience to be around. "It's our anniversary. Do you really think I'll be fooling around with another man on our anniversary trip?"

"It was a wee joke," I said. "I trust you completely."

After first looking around to be sure we were alone, he leaned in and gave me a quick kiss on the cheek, followed by a gentle hug so as not to jar my headache. "And I trust *you*," he said with a beaming smile on his handsome face.

I stepped back and scoped him out from head to foot. He wore a brand-new Yosemite T-shirt with an elk on the back, which we had purchased only yesterday in the gift shop at the Ahwahnee hotel after lunch. He had on beige hiking shorts with a hundred pockets in them and heavy hiking boots, also purchased at the hotel, lined with thick gray socks that looked about five times too big for him. Arthur's legs were pale but as beautiful and fuzzy and strong as they were the first time I saw (and fell in love with) them. His face was lit with happiness, which wasn't entirely due to the beauty of nature surrounding us, but which I'm pretty sure had something to do with the fact that upon waking in our rustic rented cabin, we had partaken of a spirited round of sex to celebrate the sun rising over the mountains outside.

He laid a fingertip on my chin to get my attention. "Get some rest. I'll be back before you know it."

I nodded, accepted another peck on the cheek, and turned to watch him head off down the trail toward the Ahwahnee, where his hiking group was going to meet up. As he walked along, he occasionally wiggled his ass for my enjoyment, simply because he knew I was watching. He also whistled a merry tune as he clomped along in his big butchass boots.

With a final turn and wave, which I returned, he disappeared around a bend in the trail, and I headed back to the cabin. I spent some time in the shower, then clad in my own hiking shorts and nothing else, I headed out to the front porch to recline in one of the gliding rockers and gaze out at the beautiful landscape surrounding me.

Neither of us had ever been to Yosemite before, and we were having a ball. I had lied about the headache, of course. I simply didn't feel like hiking up a mountain and being jovial with a bunch of strangers while I did it. Besides, I reasoned, a little time apart would be good for Arthur and me. Absence makes the heart grow fonder, and all that shit.

And truthfully, I was once again sinking into one of my discontented phases. No, not discontented, I suppose, just bored. I had noticed the boredom growing in me for a couple of years now, and to tell the truth, it confused me.

I loved Arthur. I did. Still, I couldn't help thinking my life was missing something. I was pushing fifty, and while I had kept my health and most of my hair and hadn't yet let my looks go to pot, or so everyone told me, I still couldn't convince myself that life wasn't slipping past—and I was missing a lot of excitement as it did.

Perhaps gay men are not made for monogamy, I told myself. Or perhaps *I'm* not. For Arthur didn't seem to have a problem focusing all his love on one man. Me.

Sometimes I couldn't help thinking that maybe the problem was all mine. Maybe when I boiled down all the facts, I would find the truth had settled to the bottom of the pan like sludge. And the truth, when I finally saw it there, turned out to be that I was a selfish little turd who honestly cared more about myself (and my dick) than I did anybody else, including Arthur.

While my mind analyzed that possibility, I heard footsteps approaching the cabin on the pinecone-strewn path leading in from the road. I opened my eyes and immediately jerked upright.

The young man approaching the cabin was dressed somewhat like Arthur had been when he left. Hiking boots and shorts, a wrinkled sweaty tee covering his slight chest, and a huge backpack strapped to his shoulders. His legs were deeply tanned and well-muscled, brushed as they were with a smattering of black hair that pretty much matched the hair on his head, which had been shorn close. He had a few days growth of beard smudging his cheeks and chin, and a row of beautiful white teeth shone out as he smiled broadly when he saw me open my eyes and look at him.

He stopped at the bottom of the steps leading up to the porch. "I didn't mean to wake you," he said, twisting his torso a bit to redistribute the weight of the pack on his back. There was a sprinkling of perspiration on his forehead.

The man was stunning.

"Th-that's all right. Can I help you with something?"

He smiled all the wider. "I saw you at dinner last night with your friend. Is he here?"

"No," I said. "He's hiking Half Dome with a group. I—wait a minute. I remember you too. You were sitting by yourself at the table next to us."

He nodded. "That's right. You sent me a drink."

I felt myself blush. Actually, it was Arthur who had sent him the drink. Arthur hates to see anyone dine alone. "Oh, well, it was nothing."

"I hope you don't mind, but I'd like to have a few words with you."

I blinked back my surprise, then waved a hand at the steps he was standing on. "Drop your pack and have a seat. What's on your mind? Would you like something to drink?"

He dropped the backpack at his feet and tugged a water bottle out of a side pocket. "Got my own, thanks." He took a chug and stuck the bottle back in the pack. He dropped to the top step and stretched his long legs out in front of himself.

I felt a surge of desire stutter through me. God, he was beautiful.

He apparently had come to grips with what he wanted to say, so he just went ahead and said it without beating around the bush. "You and your friend are gay, aren't you?"

"Y-yes. Why do you ask?"

Now it was his turn to blush. "I—well—I saw him headed toward the lodge just now. Then when I saw you on the porch here all by yourself, I decided to go for it. I do that sometimes."

"Go for *what?*" I asked.

He gave me a grin, which somehow managed to be cocky and self-deprecating at the same time.

He grunted his way to his feet and stepped toward me as I sat there in the glider trying to figure out what was going on. He casually positioned himself directly in front of me, and as his hand caressed the fabric of his shorts directly over his crotch, which happened to be at about my eye level, he smiled down and said, "Go for you."

It dawned on me in a burst of insight that, sweet Jesus, this wasn't one of my fantasies. This was real!

Speechless, I sat before him and felt my cock lengthen in my shorts. Just as, I immediately noticed, his was doing.

He didn't seem to think speech from me was necessary. Nor did he seem to think there was anything odd about what he was doing. He tore his gaze from me just long enough to look around the cabin grounds at his back, then turning back to face me, he pulled his T-shirt over his head and tossed it in my lap.

"Take me inside," he said.

I couldn't believe it. "What makes you think you can—"

"What?" Again he squeezed the bulge of his crotch with one hand, while he stroked his stomach with the other. There was a light sweep of hair spanning his chest and a lighter trail of fuzz leading down over his belly to his belly button and points farther south. I got a better glimpse of where that trail led when, with a flick of his fingers, he popped the button on his shorts and pulled the fly slowly apart to show a bristle of pubic hair bursting into the sunlight. He was obviously completely hard now. The outline of his cock was clearly defined beneath his shorts.

"Take me inside," he said again, his fingers dipping into that glorious bush of pubic hair as he nudged the base of what looked to be a very substantial cock just crying out for a little fresh air. "Take me inside, or I'll whip it out right here."

I tore my eyes from his dick long enough to look up into his face as he smiled down at me with that sexy grin, which seemed to have grown even sexier in the last couple of minutes.

As if I had no control over my own appendages, I felt my hand press against the hardness in my own shorts as I sat there before him.

His smile widened. "I saw that. Let's go. Inside. Now."

And I let him tug me to my feet. He pointed to the door, letting me lead the way, and as I opened the door and stepped inside, he grabbed his backpack off the steps and followed me in. I watched in wonderment as he closed the door behind himself and immediately bent to begin untying his bootlaces. I simply stood watching him, trembling a little, now, because holy fuck, I was turned on.

With his laces undone, he kicked off each boot, lifted his legs one by one to take off his socks and, without hesitation, peeled his shorts away from his body and kicked them across the room.

He stood before me in all his glory. Heavenly young body, strong cock standing erect, a light of hunger beaming in his eyes. Once again he smiled, and when he did, I felt my heart give a lunge.

"Your turn," he said. "I want to see you naked."

My hands were shaking; my knees were trembling. I merely stood there, not knowing what to do.

He gave me wink. "Or maybe you'd like me to do it for you."

And without waiting for an answer, he stepped toward me, causing his erect cock to bob up and down like a drinking heron. His eyes burrowed into mine, and he laid one hand on my waist and with the other slid the zipper down on my shorts, plucked the button free, and simply stood back to let them fall. Gravity dumped them at my feet, and the next thing I knew, we were standing facing each other, completely naked.

He studied my body. "You're sexy as hell. How old are you. Forty?"

"Ish," I said. I was forty-eight. "How old are you?"

He gave me a smile that said he knew I was fudging the numbers a bit. "Nineteen," he said, then added, "ish."

"Wow," I breathed, staring at his beauty. His youth. His magnificent dick.

He winked. "Was that a good wow or a bad wow?"

"A good wow."

"Glad to hear it," he said, gripping his cock with his fist and giving it a stroke or two for my viewing pleasure. "Now taste me."

And placing his hands on my shoulders, he applied just enough pressure to coax me to my knees before him. As my hand came up to cup his balls, he stepped toward me and put his thumb on my chin. Adding pressure there as well, he coaxed my mouth open, and when he had it the way he wanted it, he took one more step forward and pushed his cock between my lips.

I reached around to grab the back of his thighs and pull him closer as his hips pressed against me and his cock began a gentle rocking motion in my mouth. I felt his legs tremble beneath my hands, and I rested my forehead against his stomach as I relished the taste of his dick on my tongue. He must have just showered, for the scent of him was clean and flowered. He smelled and tasted yummy.

He bent to run his hands along my back, and as he did, he pulled his cock away and lowered himself to his knees before me. Taking my face in his hands, he gently laid his mouth to mine and slid his tongue in to replace where his cock had been only moments before. Even his breath was sweet. I closed my eyes and savored the taste of him.

Urging me gently to the floor, he laid me out before him, and with his hands stroking my heated body, he pushed his face into my crotch, licking my balls, then sliding his tongue upward along the shaft of my dick until, with a smile, he popped the head of it in his mouth and did some savoring of his own.

Just as my back was beginning to arch, he freed me from his mouth and deftly flipped me over onto my stomach. When he did, I lifted my ass just enough not to break my erect cock on the hardwood floor, and the moment my ass was in the air, he slid his tongue across my hole and, with puckered lips, sucked my asshole like a lollipop. As he explored the rim of my hole with his tongue, I found myself opening myself up to him even more, lifting my ass higher and grabbing my cock beneath me to stroke it as he worked his magic on my ass.

When he withdrew his mouth from me, I stayed in the position I was in, still stroking my aching cock and exposing my ass to him completely. He chuckled, and the next thing I heard was the tearing of foil. He rose up onto his knees behind me, and when I turned to see what he was doing, I saw him slide a condom over his dick and roll it down as far as it would go.

When he was satisfied, he laid a warm hand on the small of my back and leaned in to dampen my anal ring with his spit. When he had me good and moist, he again laid his tongue to my hole and teased me as I trembled beneath him.

"I'm going to fuck you now," he muttered, still slavering over my ass, and to show him I understood, I spread my legs a little wider.

I was shaking like a fucking willow tree in a windstorm as he pressed the head of his dick to my sphincter. I forced myself to relax, and a moan escaped my lips as he pushed the length of his cock slowly into me until I was stabbed to the core.

Once inside as far as he could go, he remained there, motionless, as I inured myself to his length and girth. A minute later it was I who began to move, letting him know I was comfortable enough. Laying his hot mouth to the back of my neck, he began to rock his cock in and out of me. Slowly. Oh so slowly.

He stood on his knees behind me, his back as straight as his cock, and gripping my hips, he pulled and pushed himself in and out of me. I continued to stroke my dick with one hand while reaching behind me to clutch his hip to guide his movements and steer him into me—not that he needed any help.

He moved his hands to my shoulders and held me in place as his tempo sped up, and his cock, amazingly enough, became even harder and larger inside me. After a couple of minutes of furious pounding, I knew he was getting close. And so was I.

With my face smashed into the floor, I beat my cock in a frenzy of lust as his dick continually tore a heated path through my soul.

"Fuck me," I breathed. "Sweet Jesus, fuck me."

He took a fistful of my hair and pulled my head back as his cock began stabbing me with a fury I had never felt from Arthur. The pain was exquisite.

I stammered nonsensical words and bucked beneath him, backing into every new thrust just to make it deeper.

He leaned over me and whispered in my ear, "I knew you'd be a good fuck."

And the next thing I knew, he slid his cock out of me and twisted me over onto my back beneath him. He slapped my hand away from my dick and used his own spit-dampened fist to pump the come from me. When my back rose up off the floor and the first jet of come burst from me, he bent over me and let the wash of it splatter his face. He gripped my cock and spread my juices over his face as I lay there watching and trembling beneath him.

When I was drained, he opened his eyes, and with his face dripping with my come, he straddle-walked over me, still on his knees, until his condomed cock stood directly over my face.

Looking down at me with a grin, he peeled the condom away and threw it aside. Taking his cock in his hand, he began stroking himself, all the while scraping his cockhead against my lips, my nose, my cheeks. He scooted a little farther up and pressed his balls to my mouth, and I savored them just as he had savored me.

When his knees tightened around me and his breath shortened, I pleaded, "Give it to me. Let me drink you. Please. Let me drink you."

With a childlike smile, he laid his cock against my lips and watched as I opened wide for him. He slid his dick into my mouth and immediately arched his back away from me. I reached up with both hands to stroke his stomach and chest as he gave a great gasp and grunt and suddenly emptied himself into me. Surge after surge of hot come came rushing into my mouth. I gurgled and gasped and chased every jet of it until the young man over me was as drained as I.

With a final shudder, he slid his sated cock from my lips and doubled over me like a pocketknife, hugging my head in his arms. I reached around him to hold him close as our two hearts began quieting down.

We lay that way for the longest time.

Later, as he gathered his things together and began to dress, we passed meaningless mundanities about the weather and the park. He adjusted the pack on his back and stepped through my cabin door without so much as saying good-bye, and I felt my loneliness come sliding back.

"Thank you," I said softly as I watched him walk away. Then, even more softly, I muttered, "I'm sorry, Arthur. I'm sorry."

I closed my eyes and remembered everything my young visitor and I had experienced with each other. A sadness swept in as, all over again, I felt the thrill and fear and euphoria of being lusted after by a younger man. The erotic rush of having his hands on me. I relived the feel of his iron cock buried deep inside me. I felt and tasted again his sweet, hot seed as it gushed into my hungry mouth. I felt again his mouth drinking *my* come and relishing every drop.

I felt it all. Every moment. Every lunge. Every shudder.

What I didn't feel was guilt. And that saddened me most of all.

# Chapter Six

IN MY imagination the train still hummed along the tracks, not yet slowing for the Capistrano stop.

"We'll be detraining soon," I said. "Let me just make a quick trip to the bathroom."

Arthur patted my hand and sent me along my way. Before I left, I gathered up our trash from lunch and took it with me on my way to finding the restroom facilities, which Arthur, who had been an American citizen for over twenty years, still charmingly called the loo.

Our seats were on the upper level of the car, the bathroom on the lower. At the foot of the stairs leading down, I spotted a waste receptacle and dumped the crap from lunch. A few steps farther along I found two bathrooms marked MEN and WOMEN. I ducked through the door marked MEN and closed the door behind me to find…

*…THERE WERE two stalls and two urinals. I chose the urinal closest to the wall and unleashed Davey Jr. for a much-needed whiz. The moment I was pissing freely, the bathroom door opened and in stepped the father of the two young girls I had seen and admired earlier. Close up he was even more handsome than he appeared when I saw him walking away from me down the aisle with his kids in tow. He was taller than I and had a broad, deep chest with a clump of chest hair poking out the top of the skintight T-shirt that barely had enough thread count to hide the chest at all. The T-shirt was stretched so tightly across that wide expanse of pecs that I could clearly see his nipples poking against the fabric. I felt my mouth begin to water just looking at them.*

*The man smiled broadly when I was finally able to drag my eyes from his body to his face. Giving me a friendly nod of the head and a jovial wink by way of greeting, as if he knew exactly what I was thinking, he walked straight toward me and positioned himself in front of the urinal to my right. A moment later two streams of urine merrily filled the silence.*

*He gave an ecstatic sigh, which made me grin. I was feeling precisely the same way.*

*Figuring a bit of conversation wouldn't ruin the camaraderie, I said, "I saw you with your children earlier. Are they enjoying the train ride?"*

*He turned to me and laughed. When he spoke I was surprised to hear his voice boom out of him like a foghorn. There was a smile that split his face in two, and I knew immediately I was in the presence of one of those eternally ebullient men who laugh uproariously at even the sorriest joke and whose zest for life is surpassed only by their never-ending good humor.*

*He spoke in a thick Texas accent, which was the last thing I expected. "They're having a ball! Never been on a train before. Their mother's got the little bastards reined in right now, so I've got a few minutes to myself." While my own stream of piss was beginning to dwindle down, my neighbor's seemed to have only begun. His piss was splashing the urinal like water from a fire hose smacking the side of a burning house.*

*Oddly, I found myself envying the urinal.*

*He leaned in toward me and nudged me with his elbow, while obviously still taking care to keep his stream of piss aimed in the right direction. "Nothing like a good piss to clear the pipes, huh?"*

*I laughed. "That's one way to put it." My own pipes were cleared already, but I didn't want to leave, so I just stood there, still holding my drained dick over the urinal and hoping he wouldn't notice the silence coming from my side of the pissing wall.*

*Apparently, however, he did. Peeking over the waist-high partition that separated us, he took a gander at my pecker, hanging not quite flaccid in my hand. His own dick, at the same time, began strafing its urinal with intermittent bursts of artillery fire, signaling the fact that his pipes were drawing close to being cleared as well. It took every ounce of willpower I possessed not to return the favor and peek over the partition at him.*

*"Go ahead," he said with a spark in his eye that was damned intriguing. "You know you want to look at it. Don't be shy. Take a peek. Here, I'll make it easy for you."*

*He stepped away from the urinal with one hand still holding his dick and pulled me, with my own dick still in my hand, toward him. Taking my arm, he steered me before him into the bathroom stall behind us. Once inside, there wasn't much room, what with his massive chest and our two dicks slowly filling with blood and taking up considerable room of their own.*

*He released his pecker long enough to grip me under the armpits and slowly lowered me to the toilet seat. Once there, I found myself with Tex's cock swinging half-erect only inches from my face. He looked down at me and grinned with pride like he was showing off a prize heifer.*

*"Ain't it somethin'?" he asked. "Ain't it just fucking something?"*

*It was indeed. Realizing I was at a bit of a disadvantage here if he started turning homophobe on me, I looked up past his stiffening cock to gauge the friendliness on his face. He smiled down at me with every tooth in his head flashing like neon. While I stared at his smile, his tongue came out and licked his lips. At that moment he took a tiny step closer and peeled the foreskin from his now completely erect cock back and out of the way to give me a glimpse of the glory beneath.*

*His cockhead was fat and ripe and as red as a strawberry. He dragged his own thumb over his slit to wipe away the moisture gathered there, and it was all I could do not to weep at the loss of it.*

*I ass-walked on the toilet seat to slide my trousers a little more out of my way so I could get a better grip on my own dick. When that Herculean task was accomplished, I reached*

John Inman

*up and cradled Tex's dick in my fingertips, just to get the feel of it. The second I did, the man released it and let me take control. While I hefted his fat cock in my hand to get to know it a little better, he took advantage of his two free hands to unbuckle his belt and push his trousers and underwear down around his ankles. At the same time, he tucked the tail of his T-shirt under his chin and presented himself to me in toto.*

*My god he was beautiful. Fuzzy chest, fuzzy flat belly, fuzzy long legs.*

*I leaned in and took a whiff of the man's ball sac to gauge its freshness. There was just enough of a hint of gentle sweat to make me long for more. When he took another teeny step toward me and pressed his balls to my face, I decided I'd better get down to business.*

*My friend seemed to be of the same mind.*

*He worked a finger into my mouth, and as soon as he had my lips separated, he thrust his hips forward and buried his engorged cock between my lips.*

*I had a pretty good idea where he wanted me to go with this, so I cupped his balls in one hand, and sucked his fat cock into my mouth as far as it would go, which was damn near to the root.*

*"Oh lordy," he said. "Now that's what I'm talking about. The little woman won't suck dick at all. Claims it's against her religion."*

*"Well, it isn't against mine," I mumbled around his trembling pecker.*

*"No, sir," he grinned, shaking from head to toe. "I can see it ain't."*

*Then we seemed to run out of things to talk about. He gently gripped the side of my head with his two huge hands and proceeded to facefuck me for all he was worth. While he fucked my mouth like a man on a mission, I pumped at my own dick until I was trembling every bit as much as he was.*

*The train swayed gently around us as I explored by feel the terrain of his broad chest and stomach with my free hand. Slipping my roaming hand around behind him, I felt the* smooth heat of his strong back, and when my fingers felt the swell of his ass, I dipped a finger between his fuzzy asscheeks and had the pleasure of hearing him gasp.

"Just a taste," I mumbled once again around his dick, and he obviously knew exactly what I meant.

He eased his cock from my mouth and turned to place his back to me. Clutching the coat hook on the back of the bathroom door, he leaned forward and presented that scrumptious ass to me like a waiter offering a dessert cart to a client with a sweet tooth.

I closed my eyes and breathed in the clean sweat of the man before me. When I placed my lips on his ass, I shuddered at the sensation of soft, hot flesh and hair. He repositioned his feet around mine and spread his legs wider as I took a firm grip on each of his ass cheeks and peeled them open like a grapefruit, exposing a pink hole which puckered and unpuckered as I sat there staring at it.

With one swipe of my tongue across his opening, he gave a great gasp and backed up to push his ass into my face without any preamble whatsoever. Fine by me. I went to work on his ass just as I had gone to work on his dick a couple of minutes earlier.

When he was all but going into cardiac arrest and hanging like an anchor on that poor little coat hook on the back of the door, I felt the train suddenly begin to slow around us.

Time to get this show on the road.

I gripped his hips and slowly turned him around to face me once again.

His cock was so hard it looked like it was carved from granite. A rope of precome hung off the end of it, and before I stuffed his dick back in my mouth, I extended a hungry tongue and slurped the precome away, relishing the taste.

"Oh, yes," he muttered, once again taking a gentle grip on my head to put me exactly where he wanted me. And without further ado, he stepped close and slid his cock into my hungry mouth for the final time.

*I used every trick I knew with tongue and lips on that fat, delicious cockhead, and my repertoire wasn't too shabby, if I do say so myself. In less than a minute, he arched up onto his tiptoes and started quivering like he had malaria.*

*"She's about to blow," he groaned. And a second later, she did.*

*A surging jet of come shot into my mouth as he continued to fuck my face for all he was worth. I gasped, and damned near drowned when I did. At the same moment, my own come came surging forth to match his, splashing my stomach, filling my hand.*

*"Oh, take it all," my Texan friend pleaded as he continued to pump his cock between my lips while I swallowed down everything he offered. "Drink it, sir, drink it up." I stroked his ass and pulled him all the way into me one last time as a final jet of come issued from his dick, coating my tongue.*

*"Delicious," I sighed. "Delicious. And don't call me sir."*

*"Sorry," he muttered, as he pulled his dick slowly free. "Guess I wouldn't like that either." Then to my surprise, he leaned down and buried my mouth under his in a long, lingering kiss.*

*"Just wanted to taste my come on your mouth," he said, straightening up, casually tugging his trousers up over his ass, and tucking his cock away for good.*

*God, I hated to see it go.*

SUDDENLY I realized I was alone in the toilet stall. I had always been alone.

I blinked my latest fantasy into memory with a stab of shame. Why the hell was I still doing this? What could I possibly hope to find in these imaginary trysts that I couldn't find in the real world with the man who loved me—the man who had always loved me?

I swallowed hard and fled the bathroom stall. Splashing water on my face at the sink, I studied my reflection in the mirror, not much caring for what I saw.

"Never again," I said aloud. "I mean it. Never again."

Minutes later I took my seat next to Arthur. Taking his hand, I cradled it in mine until our train swayed into the station.

IT WAS around the thirtieth year of our relationship that I began to suspect Arthur was growing bored with me. Somehow that suspicion made me want to strike out.

One summer day, a very few years into the new millennium, we were trimming the roses in our yard. While we worked, we admired the old Craftsman house Mr. B and Mr. C had left us so many long years before—the house that had been our home now for almost three decades. We had just had the house painted, inside and out, and the deep mahogany brown of the exterior was absolutely stunning. We had spent long hours together over paint charts, picking the perfect color, and now we were sprucing up the rose garden to better complement our home's new look.

I still don't understand why I felt the urge to hurt Arthur that day, but I did. And I went about it with a cool detachment that for the rest of my life I would always regret. "Have you ever cheated on me, Arthur?"

The question caught him off guard, as I knew it would. Obviously surprised, he was still unhesitant in his reply to my question, which I suddenly realized I already knew the answer to before he opened his mouth. "No," he said. "I never have. Why? Have you?"

I could feel a blush burning my cheeks. "Remember the time we rented a cabin in Yosemite? Remember the day you went for a hike to Half Dome by yourself because I said I was too tired to accompany you? A young man came to the cabin door that day, and one thing led to another."

He froze with the pruning shears in his hand. He obviously couldn't believe what he was hearing. There was an edge of growing anger in his voice, and God forgive me, it thrilled me to hear it there. "We were celebrating our twenty-fifth anniversary on that trip."

"I know," I said. "That's why I'm telling you now. I wanted to be kind and apologize."

Arthur peeled off his gardening gloves and wiped the sweat from his forehead with the tail of his shirt. His stomach was pale in the noonday sun. Arthur never liked to sunbathe. Found it too time-consuming.

The edge of anger in his words was a little sharper now. "It would have been far kinder not to have told me at all."

"Would it, Arthur?"

"You know it would."

Suddenly, I couldn't look at him. I turned again to study the house. Or I should say I turned to *pretend* to study the house.

"I always thought it would be you," he said.

That grabbed my attention. "You always thought it would be me *what?*"

Now that I was facing him, I saw the hurt in his eyes. I was pretty sure he could see the same hurt in mine. I didn't bother asking myself why *I* was feeling hurt.

"David, I always *thought* it would be you to break the trust. Your roaming eye. Your imaginary trysts with every good-looking man you see."

"How do you know about my imaginary trysts, as you call them? And besides, they're simply fantasies, Arthur. Every man has them."

"I don't."

I blinked at the way Arthur bared his soul in that one simple statement. It was like a knife turning in my chest. "Then I'm sorry," I said.

"You're sorry you cheated."

"Yes. It only happened once, Arthur. Once in thirty years."

He looked down at his feet as a tear slid down his cheek. The silence hung over us, broken only by an airliner droning across the sky above our heads, heading for a landing at Lindbergh Field with a shitload of tourists strapped inside its belly.

"You've really never cheated on me?" I asked.

"Never," he said. "Not once."

"But you're as bored as I am."

"What makes you think I'm bored?"

"Oh, come on, Arthur. I can see it in the way you look at me sometimes. I can see it in the way you move around the house. The way you pet the cat. The way you talk about work. You're bored with it all. Every piece of your life bores the crap out of you. Tell me that isn't true."

He stared at the ragged gloves in his hand, then tossed them and the clippers to the ground at his feet. Again he wiped the sweat from his forehead as he lowered himself onto the stone bench by the fence—the stone bench we had bought because it reminded us of the one in the mission garden where we first met three decades earlier.

He stared down at his hands as he began to speak. I thought I saw a slight tremor in them. His words were so soft I had to step closer to hear what he said. When I was directly in front of him, he brought out a hand and squeezed the hem of my gardening shorts between his thumb and forefinger, just to make a connection. He held onto me like that all the time his words came rushing out. I ignored the thrill I felt, even now, as the back of his fingers brushed my leg.

"I've never been bored with you, David. What you interpret as boredom is—I don't know—complacency, maybe. Just the simple act of living year after year with the same partner, in the same house, in the same city—it must all seem boring to the person looking on, I guess. But it isn't that at all. Truly." He lifted his gaze to my face. When he did, I reached down and took his hand, but he gently shook it away.

I had never known him to push me away before. Not once. My pulse thudded softly in my temples. I tried to find a way out of this mess I had dropped us both into, but I knew no matter what I did, I would never be able to make it completely right.

Arthur would never look at me the same again.

He stared up at me with a quizzical expression. There was no hatred in his glance. No anger. Just a simple need to understand. "Why did you tell me this, David? What purpose did you think it would serve to hurt me like this?"

I swallowed hard and dropped to my knees before him, cradling his hands in mine and not giving him a chance this time to pull away. "I wanted to be honest. I've felt guilty about it since it happened. I guess I just couldn't live with the guilt any longer. I—I thought you'd want to know."

It was a lie, and I knew it. It didn't take a genius to figure out Arthur knew it too.

He studied my face for the longest time before speaking. Another plane flew over our heads and disappeared in the distance before he finally found the words he wanted to say.

"This is so like you, David. You can be selfish, you know. Selfish with your time. Selfish with your heart. The only time you aren't selfish is when it benefits you. To ease your guilt over cheating on me half a dozen years ago, you risk breaking my heart just to lift the guilt from your own."

"I wanted to clear the air."

"No," he said. "You wanted to hurt me. Why?"

My throat constricted at the pall of pain in his pale blue eyes. His hair was damp with perspiration. It was a hot day. His tears had stopped flowing as quickly as they came. But more disconcerting than the missing tears was the fact that he no longer even seemed to be angry. He looked simply—tired.

"I'm sorry," I said. "I don't know why I said it. I don't know why I told you. It didn't mean anything, you know, being with that boy. It was just that, for once in my life, the fantasy was *me*. Do you understand? I was the one being wanted that time. I was the one being lusted after. Other than that it didn't mean *anything*," I said again.

A weary smile lifted the corners of Arthur's mouth. "Very little means anything to you, David. That's the problem."

"That's not true."

He tilted his head and studied me like a father witnessing the desperate lies of a child. "It is true, and you know it." He ran a fingertip along the hair on my forearm, sweaty and sprinkled with dirt as it was. When he reached my wrist with the fingertip, he slipped his hand around it and held it tight, pulling my hand to his chest where I could feel his heart thudding behind his chest.

"I forgive you, David. If it makes you happy, I forgive you. Is that what you wanted to hear me say?"

I nodded. "I'll never do it again," I said.

"No, I don't suppose you will."

"And do you still—?"

"Do I still what, David? Do I still love you?"

"Y-yes. Do you still love me?"

"Please don't ask questions you already know the answer to. Maybe you should be asking yourself the more important question."

"And what question is that?" I asked, knowing already.

"Ask yourself if you love *me*, David. Ask yourself if you really—love—me."


I STEPPED through the front door to find smoke so thick I couldn't see Sylvester until I stepped on his tail. With a horrifying wail, he tore across the room and dove under the couch. My heart was doing pretty much the same thing— bouncing around inside my chest like a terrified cat.

*Was the house on fire? What the fuck was going on?*

"Arthur!" I bellowed. "Where are you? What's burning?"

I raced into the kitchen and found a cast iron skillet on the stove with black smoke billowing out and what looked to be the cremated remains of a pound of bacon lying in the bottom of it. I snatched at the stove handle to turn off the flame beneath the skillet, but the stove top was so hot I had to waste time grabbing a dish towel off the rack by the sink to protect my hands.

With the burner finally off, I furiously slapped a lid on the skillet to slow the billowing smoke. With my hand still protected by the dish towel, I picked up the skillet and dumped it in the kitchen sink—in case the grease still decided to burst into flames. Then I stomped around from one kitchen window to the other, flinging the lot of them open wide, letting in clean air to dispel the smoke. Once the windows were open and the smoke began to thin, I traipsed through the rest of the house, room by room, opening all the windows there too.

With the air beginning to clear and my pulse slowing down to where I decided maybe I wouldn't have a stroke after all, I set off in search of Arthur.

I found him on the deck off the master bedroom. He was lying on the chaise lounge with a book splayed open across his chest, sound asleep. I collapsed against the doorframe and just stood there staring at him. Jesus what was I going to do? Arthur's memory was getting worse. He would go for days and days without an incident of forgetting, but then, like now, he would do something that actually put our lives in danger. Did I need to hire a nurse to watch over him? How could I do that? It would break his heart.

No, I decided, I would just have to watch him more closely myself. And maybe disconnect the stove. What other choice did I have? We could cook with the microwave. Couldn't we?

I stepped quietly onto the deck and stood over Arthur's chair, looking down at him. He was softly snoring, and there was a gentle smile on his face. The book splayed out across his chest was *Winnie the Pooh*, an age-old copy he had owned since childhood. It was one of his most prized possessions.

His strawberry-gray hair was tossed by the breeze blowing across the deck. I dipped my fingers in it and felt it's softness against my skin. Leaning down, I laid my lips to Arthur's ear and whispered, "Time to wake up."

His pale eyelashes fluttered. He took a firmer grip on the book beneath his hand. And with a tiny intake of breath, he opened his eyes and gazed up at me. His smile was instantaneous.

"Hi, baby," he cooed.

"Hi," I said, stroking his cheek. "Are you all right?"

He seemed surprised by the question. "Why wouldn't I be?" His eyes opened wider, and he turned his head toward the house. "I smell smoke."

"It's all right," I said. "You left the skillet on, but I took care of it."

He jumped to his feet. "Oh God. Breakfast. I was cooking breakfast."

I gave him a tsk of commiseration. "Arthur, it's four o'clock in the afternoon."

His eyes dimmed with confusion. "No. That's imposs—" He squinted into the sky above our heads and saw the sun riding the western crest of the rooftops in the distance.

"No," he said again. He heaved himself out of the chaise, dropping *Pooh* on the seat behind him, and took off toward the kitchen. I followed him across the bedroom and down the hall. At the kitchen doorway, he stopped. Flapping his hand in front of his fact to thin the stench of burnt grease and the remaining smoke, he stared at the mess in front of him. The grease-splattered stove, still smoking from the heat, the blackened skillet lying like a dead thing in the kitchen sink. The occasional drip of water leaking from the faucet hissing as it hit the heated metal beneath it. The rashers of bacon, as black as charcoal, lying in the sludge of grease which had spilled out into the sink when I dumped the skillet there.

"You've made a mess," he said, turning to me. "You've made a fucking mess."

I blinked back shock and simply stood there staring at him. Finally, I swallowed my anger and nodded my head. Beaten down with sorrow, I said softly, "I know. I'm sorry. I'll clean it up."

Arthur smiled then. "Don't look so guilty, David. I'll help you clean up the mess."

"Th-thank you," I stuttered.

Stepping around him quickly so he wouldn't see the tears beginning to fill my eyes, I grabbed the paper towels and a bottle of spray cleaner and went to work.

With a jovial slap on the butt, Arthur joined in to help.

I made a mental note to call the gas company and have the stove disconnected. I would worry later about how to explain it to Arthur.

Not that I needed to worry at all, apparently. For two seconds later, the drama and the mess and the wasted pound of bacon were completely forgotten, at least in Arthur's mind. I knew this because, even as I continued to flap a dishtowel in front of the kitchen window to ease out a little more of the hovering smoke and the reek of the ruined skillet, Arthur turned to me with an odd little pout.

After a heartbeat of silence, he waved his hand in front of his face and cried, "Aunt Tessie's bloomers, David! What's with all the fucking smoke?"


WITH THE coastal city of San Juan Capistrano less than two hours from San Diego by rail, it was still morning when we stepped from the train. The day was warm, but not overly so. It was perfect weather, in fact, for sightseeing. The California sun periodically ducked behind a scattering of high clouds to cool the air. Every time it did, a fresh breeze that felt a little like heaven slipped across my skin.

On the other side of the tracks from where we disembarked was a roadway lined with rickety shacks and clapboard houses painted in garish colors, each and every one of them geared to the tourist trade. This was the historic Los Rios area of San Juan Capistrano. There were outdoor restaurants, where tourists sat sipping tea and enjoying the shade of willow and pepper trees, trying to ignore the flies buzzing around their heads. There were other storefronts too, cluttered stalls that sold knick-knacks and mission memorabilia and just about anything a tourist might be likely to grab up and cherish and be willing to pay five times the going rate for, just to prove he had been here.

Arthur and I stood on the debarking side of the railroad tracks and stared across at Los Rios, promising ourselves later we would return and have lunch there. For now, we turned our backs on the milling street life before us and set off across the more staid and respectable Capistrano business district, heading for the old mission.

If I remembered right, it was less than a ten-minute walk away.

"I don't remember this place at all," Arthur said, studying the modern buildings and high-end businesses surrounding us, a far cry from the rustic shops and eateries on the other side of the tracks. There was sadness on Arthur's face as he repeated himself. "Why did we come here? Honestly, David, I don't remember this place at all. Are you sure we got off at the right stop? Or am I just losing my memory?"

That was the first time in a long while Arthur had admitted such a thing to me, or possibly even to himself. It saddened me to hear him say the words, but I had to laugh too, because he was absolutely right. I didn't remember the place either.

"Arthur, that's because the last time we were here, it was forty years ago, and this city looked totally different then. They've upgraded, dammit, and I don't remember any of this either."

Arthur blinked in surprise. Then he appeared considerably relieved. "Really? Well, that's not so bad, then. No reason for things not to change after forty years, I guess. God knows we have."

I laughed and bumped him with my shoulder as we strolled along. "Yes, but we changed in the opposite direction, going from young to decrepit. This city went from dumpy to classy. At least on this side of the tracks."

Arthur led me around a corner and up ahead in the distance we saw it—the old mission walls of crumbling adobe brick, and in the distance beyond that, the partial shell of the old mission cathedral, or what was left of it after the earthquake that shook it to pieces, killing forty Native American worshippers more than two centuries earlier. I had always wondered if that earthquake in 1812 which buried those forty worshippers in the rubble of the toppled church had put a wee damper for a while on the enthusiasm of the Native Americans to have their souls saved by the fucking white men. Or had they merely seen it as a divine prank—a less-than-forgiving God testing His new converts in the limits of their adopted faith?

Arthur suddenly stopped in midstride, dragging me to a halt beside him. "Wait a minute," he said, almost breathlessly sighing the words. "Now that I see the mission walls, I *do* remember. Something about the curve of the street, the uphill grade, the three-way crossing. It's brought it all back. I remember walking down this street holding your hand. It was just before… just before…." He turned and stared along the sidewalk we had just traveled. And then a beatific smile lit his face, erasing the years, erasing the confusion. "Just before we made love for the very first time. In a big old house. A house back there on that rundown little street with all the shops and restaurants on it."

I found myself nodding, hanging on to every word he uttered. When he finally turned his bright eyes back to me, I grinned. "It was an old Victorian bed and breakfast. You had an upstairs room. I followed you there."

He laid his hand over his heart as if to still its hammering. His eyes opened wide. "I *dragged* you there. You were so excited, you came before I got your clothes off. Remember how embarrassed you were?"

I groaned, then laughed. "I was appalled. It was the worst moment of my life."

"And the best moment of mine. It was the sexiest thing I'd ever seen. And I told you so." He blinked, studying my face. "Didn't I? Didn't I tell you that?"

"Yes," I said. "And I don't believe it now any more than I believed it then."

His eyes narrowed, still remembering. "I went down on you then. I dropped to my knees in front of you, peeled off your clothes, and licked the come away. You were so beautiful. Your skin was speckled in shadow from the lace curtains because it was broad daylight. Remember? Your legs were trembling as you stood there before me, your hands in my hair. Even after coming, you were still hard. You tasted delicious. You *still* taste delicious."

I laughed. "I think you're romanticizing a bit."

His eyes grew serious. A stubborn tilt, which I knew all too well, straightened his jawline. "No, David. I'm not romanticizing at all. That's exactly how it happened." He plucked at my sleeve as we stood there in the middle of the street while countless other tourists and shoppers flowed around us, politely ignoring the two old farts blocking traffic. "Please tell me you remember, David. Please tell me that moment meant as much to you as it still means to me."

I ignored the souls gliding past and reached out to lay my hand on Arthur's shoulder. "I remember," I softly said. "Don't worry. I remember every minute of that day. That weekend. I think of it all the time."

His eyes lit up. "Do you?"

"Yes. Now come on. Let's go see the mission."

He nodded acquiescence, and scooping his arm through mine, I steered him toward the mission entrance. As we stepped through the doorway out of the sun and into the cool shade of the lobby area, he pointed to a sign. "Wow," he whispered. "It costs sixteen bucks to get in. I think it was seventy-five cents the last time we were here."

"Yeah," I smirked. "*Forty years ago.*"

He laughed and said, "You pay. I got it last time."

THE SUN had momentarily dipped behind the clouds again, and looking up I realized the clouds were darker now. Was a rain squall moving in from the ocean? Were we about to get our heads wet? Slowly, however, the day again brightened around us as the clouds thinned once more. Still I kept a wary eye overhead as I followed Arthur along the paths leading toward the central courtyard.

The grounds of the mission at San Juan Capistrano were well tended but stirred no memories inside me. The courtyard, which had been a riot of color and blooming beauty forty years ago, was now daubed with the sepia tones of dry earth and chaparral. Arthur noticed it too.

"Where are the tulips? I remember tulips. Of every color in the rainbow. And the hanging wisteria! There were walls of it before. Do you remember? There was a purple wisteria on that wall over there and also among the grapevines in that arbor by the wine vats."

I was impressed. *Good lord. He's remembering more than I do.*

"Yes, Arthur. I believe you're right." I studied the grounds more closely. Even the grassy areas were faded and brittle. The courtyard was still beautiful, but in a more rustic way. What color was left was muted, dimmed. Almost—

"Sad," Arthur said. "It looks sad."

I laid my hand to his back as we continued to follow the path we were on, which led to the fountain at the courtyard's center. There was color there, at least, the greens and yellows of lily pads and water life floating on the pool. As we neared we saw flashes of gold and orange and white beneath the water. Koi. They followed us as we ambled around the fountain. Arthur dipped his hand in the water and an orange beauty rose to nip softly at his fingers, making him laugh and jerk his hand away.

We stopped, studying the lily pads, the blooms, the flashes of koi beneath the sparkling water.

"I think they've gone desert," I said. "With the landscaping, I mean. These are all indigenous plants, Arthur. Desert shrubbery. I guess even the great Mission of San Juan Capistrano has to conserve water and try to save on their utility bill. What better way to do it than rip up all the water guzzling flowers and replace them with desert foliage?"

Arthur nodded. "Yes," he said softly. "But it's still beautiful, don't you think? After all, the mission hasn't changed. Just the grounds."

I smiled at the hopefulness on his face. Even while I cried a bit inside for the loss of color, I had to agree the place was still magnificent. What had been hanging drapes of blue wisteria on the high adobe walls overlooking the tallow vats and tanning area had been replaced by climbing banks of green ivy. Still lovely, just not as vivid to behold.

"I think I like the new look better," I said, trying to bolster his enthusiasm, as well as my own. "It's more—*historical.*"

"Yeah!" he agreed, eager-eyed. "It looks like it probably looked two hundred years ago. Where in the hell would the old priests get tulip bulbs anyway? They didn't have a Home Depot close by."

And the next thing I knew we were giggling like a couple of school kids. Arthur dipped his hand in the fountain again, and when a particularly friendly koi with black and orange streaks crawling down its back took a nip at him, Arthur squealed and yanked his hand out of the water so fast he splashed us both, which made us giggle all the more. When I noticed a few somber and staid tourists eyeing us askance, as if maybe they thought we were heathens or something, I tugged Arthur away toward a gateway at the north end of the courtyard, just to make our escape.

Once through the gate, Arthur stopped so fast I plowed right into him. He was staring straight ahead with a stunned expression on his face. I turned to see what he was staring at and saw a tiny enclosed area, roofless and barren of adornments except for four great bells hanging in niches in a low adobe wall. But it wasn't the bells Arthur found so fascinating. It was the stone bench that abutted another grape arbor.

He stepped toward it almost like a worshipper approaching a holy site. At the bench he stopped and ran his fingers over the stone. His smile returned, and I tore my eyes from it to look at the map they had given us at the front gate. Looking around to try to place myself inside the map, I realized we had entered what was called the Sacred Garden.

"What?" I asked, still confused. "What is it?"

Arthur turned to me, and I was surprised to see tears streaming down his cheeks, but the tears were belied by a wondrous smile that had spread his lips. With that smile softening his features, he once again looked like he had the very first time I laid eyes on him.

"Here," he fiercely whispered, pulling me close. When I was by his side, he bent and patted the stone bench. He looked up at me like a teacher trying to get a particularly stupid student to grasp quantum physics. "I was right here," he said again, enunciating every syllable as if he wasn't sure I understood English at all. "I was sitting right here when you came up to me that day. *It was right here that we spoke to each other for the very first time.*"

I blinked back my surprise, then gave my full attention to the bench, the walls, and Arthur's excited smile still beaming from him like a floodlight, spraying me with a desperate longing. Suddenly forty years fell away, and that day came flooding back. I began to nod. Then I felt my lips begin to stretch wide as my smile rose up to match Arthur's.

"My God, Arthur, I think you're right!"

He stepped into my arms. "It was here that I fell in love with you. Right here in this very spot."

I gave him an incredulous chuckle. "Okay, now, let's not get *too* fanciful in our romanticizing. Nobody falls in love that fast, Arthur. Nobody. You might fall in lust maybe, but love?"

Still in my arms, he pulled away just far enough to glower at me. "Don't tell *me* when I fell in love. I guess I know better than you do, don't I?"

I cringed beneath his stare, but still I was smiling. "Sorry I spoke. Okay. I believe you. This is where you fell in love with me."

He seemed satisfied that I had accepted the truth of it without him having to resort to fisticuffs to get it through my thick skull. He stepped from my embrace, but only enough for one arm to leave me. The other arm still draped across my back. I felt his fingers on my shoulder. His leg against my leg.

"We should have married here," he said.

I rolled my eyes. "Not sure they'd have let us. Catholics, you know. Not exactly up on marriage equality."

Arthur laughed. "Well, then, fuck 'em."

Once again, he turned to study my face. "I wonder if that B&B where I was staying forty years ago is still in business."

I narrowed my eyes. "W-why would you be wondering that?"

But instead of answering, he suddenly gazed at the clouded sky above our heads, then toward the adobe walls surrounding us.

"Wait a minute," he said, a furrow digging its way into his forehead.

"What, Arthur? What's wrong *now*?"

He cocked his head as if listening for an expected sound. But obviously it wasn't there.

"Where are the swallows?" he asked. "Where are the goddamn swallows?"


"THEY'RE GONE," I said. "You know that, Arthur. The swallows don't come to the mission anymore. They've taken up new digs somewhere else."

Arthur wore a horrified expression, like someone who has just been told his pet Pekingese is actually an alien from another planet and now it's time for him to fly back home. "What the fuck are you talking about, David? Everyone knows the swallows come to San Juan Capistrano every year. There's a song about it and everything. Hell, look over there."

We were even now ambling along one of the trails twisting through the old mission grounds. Arthur pulled me up short and pointed to a sign not ten feet in front of us. The sign read, "Swallows Viewing Station." He waited until he was sure I had read it, then stuck his fist on his hip, and said, "See?"

I donned my patient face, even while I felt that old familiar sadness rising up inside me once again—that sadness that told me Arthur would be leaving me one day. Or at least his mind would.

I took his hand, "Baby, we had this conversation a few years ago. I guess you've forgotten. The swallows don't come here anymore. Their migratory path has changed. It has something to do with the mission walls being repaired, and in the process the old swallows' nests were destroyed. I suppose the birds figured they weren't welcome any more. They've moved on, Arthur. They've found a different home. I guess the mission people just haven't gotten around to changing their signs yet. Maybe they're living in denial."

Arthur gave me the look of a man who knows he's being conned. Then he tilted his head and gave me a playful slap on the cheek. "You're talking out of your ass, love." A second later he was once again tugging me down the path. "Come on," he said. "Let's go see the chapel."

As we walked I saw his eyes continually stray to the eaves of the mission walls. He was obviously still searching for swallows.

"They're gone," I said softly.

And Arthur laughed. "Oh, shut up."

I sighed. Arthur would just have to come to grips with the truth in his own sweet time. In the meantime he pulled me toward the chapel doors.

"I thought you quit church," I said.

He hooked his thumb over his shoulder, obviously indicating San Diego behind us. "I quit *that* one, not *this* one. I quit *church*, not God."

"Ah. I see."

Stepping into the cool darkness of the Serra Chapel was like stepping into an oasis. The pews were roughhewn wood, the floors uneven flagstone, the walls adorned with grim religious paintings. The altar and the wall behind it were of a gleaming golden hue, ornate, sparkling, peopled with effigies of figures from both the Bible and the real world, including Father Junipero Serra, the founder of the mission. The inside of the chapel was even dimmer than I remembered it. Probably because of the cloudy skies outside. The last time Arthur and I had been here, four decades earlier, the sun had been out in full force, and stepping into the shadowed chapel then had rendered one almost sightless.

"It's just as I remember it," Arthur said, surprising me. His voice was hushed in deference to the sanctity of the hall surrounding us.

As he pulled me into a pew near the front, the back of the pew in front of us cool and smooth beneath my hand, I matched him whisper for whisper. "Are you saying you remember this place? You haven't seen it for forty years."

We were sitting side by side now, and he leaned toward me, discreetly taking my hand. "How could anyone forget this place? You know, I was sitting here for the longest time that day. That day you came up to me in the garden. I don't remember what I was praying for, David, but I think God knew anyway. I was praying for some love to come into my life. And not ten minutes later, He sent me you."

The beauty of the old chapel hovered on the outskirts of my vision as I studied Arthur's face. The gentle smile. The absolute knowledge in his eyes that the words he spoke were true. And the loving way those eyes regarded me beside him.

His thumb slid across the palm of my hand as I felt my eyes mist up. "I've loved you since that day," he said. "I haven't stopped even once."

I swallowed the lump in my throat. Where had that come from? "I'm sorry I haven't always been what you needed. I'm sorry I haven't always given you what you deserved."

Arthur's face softened even more. "You still love me, don't you?"

"Yes," I said. "Even when I thought I didn't."

"Then that's all I've asked. Now hush. I want to pray."

I sat silently as Arthur kneeled on the flagstone floor and rested his forehead on the cool wooden pew in front of us. I watched him closely. His lips did not move. Devoted words were not whispered aloud. But I knew in my heart that Arthur was truly lost in prayer. There was always such goodness and truth in him, I never doubted it for a minute.

I also knew that a fairer God would not have given Arthur to me at all. I didn't deserve him. I had *never* deserved him.

While Arthur prayed, I laid my hand on his back and stared through the chapel's side door as scattered raindrops began sprinkling the earthen walkway outside. The rain cooled the air in the chapel even more. While Arthur prayed, I closed my eyes and relished the feel of it on my skin. I also savored the feel of Arthur's back beneath my hand, the gentle intake of his breath, the absolute stillness of his body in worship.

Enjoying these things was, I knew, about as close to prayer as I would ever get. And I didn't mind at all, because they made me happy.

Arthur. Arthur made me happy. And it had taken my whole life to realize that if anyone was making me miserable, it was myself. But had I made Arthur miserable too? Even a little bit?

God, I hoped not.

WE SAT at one of the outdoor restaurants in Los Rios, on the far side of the tracks, just as the day began darkening to night. Since we had planned on making our excursion a day trip, we had an hour to kill before our train arrived to carry us back to San Diego. I figured the train couldn't come soon enough because already the scattered raindrops were skittering down the backs of our necks.

Arthur didn't seem to care about the threat of a little rain, and he certainly wasn't in any sort of hurry as he piddled around sipping his iced tea and poking at his dinner.

Ever since we left the chapel, his face had been composed with such an expression of peace and contentment, it was hard to argue with the old adage that prayer eases a troubled heart. There was such a gentle radiance in his eyes as he looked at me now that I was beginning to find myself aroused, just as I had been aroused on that long ago day when those same azure eyes touched me for the very first time.

"I love this air," Arthur said, and I watched as he closed his eyes and leaned his head back, savoring the breeze on his face, the wind in his hair. If the air threatened rain, it didn't seem to bother Arthur at all.

I smiled, watching him. "You've never been more handsome than you are right now."

His soft smile widened. His eyes opened just enough for him to study me through the blond haze of his long pale lashes. He moved his lips to the words "Thank you," but no sound came out. Then he gave himself a shake as if leaving his reverie behind and leaned toward me across the table.

"I know what's happening, you know."

For a moment I honestly didn't know what he meant.

Then he made it crystal clear. "I remember what the doctor told us, David. I have Alzheimer's, don't I? Isn't that what he said? I can feel things slipping away from me. It began with random words that wouldn't come. Then one day I turned around and couldn't remember what I had been doing five minutes earlier. Now those immediate memories are sometimes still there and sometimes not. I never know what I'll remember five minutes hence." His face creased into a melancholy smile as he watched me. "Like this moment right now. It breaks my heart to think I'll forget it the minute we step away from this table." He said the horrible words again. "I have Alzheimer's, don't I." It wasn't a question. It was stated as fact.

And it was totally wrong.

"No, Arthur, you don't. You are in the beginning stages of dementia. Like we explained to you before. It's just a little memory loss. The doctor said you have years and years of normal living left before it becomes—debilitating. If it ever really does."

I knew I was on the verge of lying to avoid the truth, so I forced myself to stop talking. The pain was too great to continue until I took a deep breath and sat stone still for a moment to let the cool evening air, dampened with rain, flow over *my* face, just as Arthur had let it flow over his.

I only opened my eyes when Arthur took my hand in his atop the table. "How *many* years?" he asked. "How *many* years before I wake up one day and find a stranger sleeping next to me?"

Biting back a frown, only because I didn't want him to see my anguish, I dragged up a smile instead from some long-forgotten well of imagination I apparently still held at my disposal. It didn't make me feel any better, and judging by the hurt in Arthur's eyes, it didn't make him feel any better either.

Still, a smile, more honest than mine softened his features. "You always were a terrible liar, David. You wear the truth on your face like other men wear a beard. I can always read what you're thinking. Did you know that?"

This time my smile was honest enough, even while my heart still ached inside. "I suspected as much."

Still holding hands, we let the rain-soaked air blow our sorrow away. We listened in silence to the hum of the voices of other diners surrounding us, their tones growing a little more angsty as the rain began to strengthen. This was Southern California, after all. There wasn't an umbrella in sight. People never seemed to think it would rain here.

"We still have time," I said, stroking the back of Arthur's pale hand with my thumb, causing a jolt of sexual awakening to course through me. "We have a long time to still have each other completely, you and I. It's only the little things you'll forget. The immediate things. Our past will always be with you, just as it will always be with me. You won't lose it, Arthur. Not for a long, long time. If ever."

I watched in silence as a lone tear slid down his cheek to sparkle at his jawline. Or was it a raindrop?

"Do you promise?" he whispered fiercely. "I don't want to miss our happy ending, David. I've invested too much time in it. I've centered my whole life around you. You can't slip into the shadows now. Promise me."

And I nodded back. Just as fiercely as his whisper. "I promise, baby. If you lose sight of where we are, I'll always be there to point the way. I'll always be there to remind you that you're mine. And I'm yours. I won't let you slip away either, Arthur. If you ever did, what would I have left? What would there be left in this life to love if you weren't here with me?"

He eased his hand from mine and picked up his fork to play some more with his food. "There were times over the years that I thought you hated me."

And somehow, I couldn't hold the words back. I let them fall. "There were times over the years that I thought I did too. I don't understand it, Arthur. I'll never understand it. Put that fucking fork down and take my hand." He did as I asked. When his warm, strong hand was once again engulfed in mine, I said, "I'm sorry I made you feel unloved. I think it was aging that got to me. A midlife crisis maybe. Whatever. The fear of not being wanted any more. The fear of not being hungered for."

Arthur gave me a cluck of sympathy. "Have you been as blind as all that? I have always hungered for you."

I grinned. "I know."

He leaned close and reached out his free hand to rest it on the side of my face. "As long as I'm alive on this planet, David, you will never be unloved."

I tilted my head into his hand, ignoring the gaze of a child studying us from one of the surrounding tables. "I know that too, Arthur. Deep down I've always known it."

"And the other men? All those young, gorgeous men you fantasized about? How did they fit in? And the others too. The ones who maybe *weren't* fantasies, but were flesh and blood and passion. What about those men?"

Suddenly, with those simple words, my guilt came flooding back. Guilt for that one weak moment when I didn't have the strength to turn away from what was being offered. I knew I had to explain. I had to make him understand.

"I told you the truth when I told you it only happened once. Please don't think I spent my life cheating on you. I didn't. That time at Yosemite was my only act of infidelity."

"No, David. You tell yourself it was, but that isn't true. In my mind, every one of those fantasies you lived inside your head was an act of infidelity too. But don't look so sad. I also know if I have to choose between my husband cheating on me in real time, or cheating on me inside his head, I'll take door number two any day. It just hurts is all. It still hurts, even though I know it isn't true. It meant your eye strayed from me, you see. It meant I wasn't enough to always hold your gaze."

I spotted something through the surrounding foliage. Something in the distance. My God, I couldn't believe it.

And before I knew what was happening, I heard a laugh. The laugh was mine.

"If you think you didn't hold my gaze all these years, Arthur, then maybe the dementia has already knocked the sense out of your head. You held my gaze all right. You not only held my gaze, you held my heart. I'm sorry it has taken me so long to fully realize that fact. But I intend to make it up to you, all those years of wanting what I didn't have and ignoring what I had. All those years of thinking I didn't have enough. Or that I could do better. Or that I wasn't being loved the way I should have been loved."

Arthur was smiling now. He had a mischievous gleam in his eye. He was playing along. Playing along just as he always did when he thought I had something up my sleeve. "How?" he asked. "How do you intend to make it up to me?"

I waved to the waitress for the check without taking my eyes from Arthur's face. "Let me just pay this goddamn bill, then come with me, Arthur. Come with me right now, and I'll show you."

Arthur checked his watch. "But we have a train to catch."

I gave him a wink and what I hoped was a sexy little smile. "Fuck the train."

"What's that supposed to mean?"

"I think we should stay over."

Arthur blinked. I'm not sure if he was blinking in surprise or blinking back a raindrop. "Stay over *where*?"

"Here," I said, digging for my credit card to hand to the waitress, who had shown up with our tab in hand. I tapped Arthur's arm. "Look."

I pointed through the branches of the pepper tree we were sitting under. The moment I did, I realized the rain had increased and it was only because of the thick foliage of the tree hanging over our heads that we hadn't noticed.

Both Arthur and the waitress aimed their gaze at the gap in the foliage I was pointing at. And at the old Victorian house exposed in the distance.

"It's your bed and breakfast, Arthur. It's still in business. Look," I said again. I could see the sign. I could see a wet flag hanging limp on a pole sticking out over the front door.

Arthur swiveled in his chair. His eyes lit up. I could almost feel the memories stirring in his head. "My God," he breathed. "That's it! That's where we stayed forty years ago."

I tugged at his sleeve to bring his gaze back to me. "And that's where we'll stay tonight, if they have a vacancy."

Arthur's eyes sparkled bright. "Really? You mean it?"

"I'll get us a room come hell or high water."

"Don't worry," the waitress interrupted. "That's Alice's bed and breakfast. Alice is my sister." She leaned in close and plucked the credit card from my hand. With a conspiratorial twinkle in her eyes, she said with a wink, "Take my word for it, boys. Alice has a vacancy."

# Chapter Seven

THE MAN standing behind the counter of the bed and breakfast appeared to be about twenty years old. He had black hair that hung to his shoulders, a tiny dangling crucifix in one ear, Rasta beads around one wrist, and a T-shirt that was three sizes too small. The tee was so short that when I leaned over the counter to talk to him, I could cast my eyes downward and see a treasure trail of dark hair cascading down from his belly button to the top of his low-slung blue jeans.

"Stop it," I mumbled to myself, nipping my fantasy in the bud. "You're a married man. Act like one."

THE YOUNG clerk jumped like I had poked him with a pin. "I'm sorry, sir. What did you say?"

I tugged out my wallet and slid my credit card and ID across the counter. Trying to fight back a blush, I answered, "Nothing, son. Nothing. Just talking to myself. It's a privilege old people take full advantage of every chance they get."

He offered up an uncomfortable cluck of either sympathy or confusion—I wasn't sure which. "Uh, okay," he said, still trying to be nice even in the face of such blatant insanity. "If you say so."

A moment later, my credit verified and paperwork complete, I found Arthur waiting for me in the rose garden at the side of the B&B. Because no one loves rose gardens more than Arthur does, I had suspected that was where he would be. The rain was gathering strength now. The roses, in a dozen blazing colors, were bobbing and shuddering on the end of their stems as the raindrops peppered down on top of their heads. Their scent was sweet on the rain-dampened air.

Delicious. Arthur's hair was soaking wet, his shirt stuck to his chest. He didn't seem to mind at all. He had a grin on his face that stretched from one ear to the other. That was pretty delicious too.

"I got it," I said.

He did a little tap dance in the mud. The look of wonder in his eyes made me grin. Impossibly, his smile spread wider than it already was.

"The same room?" he asked. "You got the same room?"

I pointed to the outside staircase, rickety with age, buried in ivy, climbing to a tiny porch and doorway on the second floor with a wind chime hanging from the eave depicting circling birds tinkling merrily in the gusts of rain-soaked air. "It's right up there." I said. "Remember?"

Arthur's eyes followed where I was pointing, and as he gazed up the stairs, he brought his hand to his chest, as if trying to corral his galloping heart.

"My God," he breathed. "You're right. That's the room. That's where it was. There wasn't any ivy then, or a wind chime, but that's the place. I can't believe it."

It was at that precise moment that the rain let loose with a *whoosh*, nailing us both. A boom of distant thunder made us jump in our tracks. Laughing and hooting like a couple of kids, we rushed toward the steps and the tiny porch at the top of it to duck in out of the rain.

It seemed strange to be climbing up to that rented room empty-handed. We didn't have so much as a toothbrush between us, but I didn't care. Halfway up the staircase, Arthur reached around behind him, took a firm grip on my hand, and pulled me the rest of the way like a kid dragging his mother into an ice-cream shop.

By the time we reached the landing, we were completely drenched and giggling like fools.

I had never been so in love in my life, I suddenly realized. But then I did a mental head slap and realized I most certainly had. My *whole* long life.

With Arthur. It had always been with Arthur.

The raindrops beat a tattoo on the little porch's tin roof that sounded like a chorus line of tap dancers hoofing it over our heads. Arthur reached out with a fingertip and stroked one of the wind chime's ceramic birds tinkling and spinning in circles. "Look," he said. "Swallows." Then he took the room key from my hand, and with a deep breath of expectation, he opened the door before us.

Arthur snaked his arm through mine as we stepped inside.

"Husbands," I whispered to no one but myself, just because at that particular moment in time, I needed to hear the word. It sounded exactly right inside my head, even if Arthur *didn't* hear me utter it. He was too engrossed in what lay through the doorway to listen to my insane ramblings.

I heard him gasp.

And I have to admit, I gasped too at the sight of the old room. So many memories flooded in, I almost lost my balance.

It was Arthur's steadying hand and Arthur's voice that brought me back. Just as it always did.

"Nope," he groused, casting a critical eye from one corner of the room to another, from bed to chair to bureau. "It's all different. Where are the lace curtains and the mountain of throw pillows on the bed? Where is the little square of carpet in the middle of the floor? And what the hell is that? That wasn't here forty years ago." He pointed to a stainless steel minibar perched atop an antique chest of drawers. It sat there looking as out of place among all the Victorian furnishings as a hooker at high tea.

Again I was mesmerized by Arthur's ability to remember facts from decades earlier but forget what he was doing five minutes earlier. He still seemed to understand what we were doing in this room, however. That memory hadn't escaped him yet. Our past was still very much inside his head. Just as it was in mine.

I laughed and stepped up behind him to fold him in my arms. Looking over his shoulder, I began pointing out items that *hadn't* changed. "It's still the same four-poster bed. It's still the same fireplace on the wall there by the big brocaded chair that, by the way, is also the same."

Arthur followed my pointing finger. "Is it? I don't remember."

"The fireplace too," I continued. "The screen is new, but the fireplace was there before. Remember?"

He nodded and leaned back into me. I felt him shudder in my arms. "I'm cold," he said.

I suddenly realized I was cold too. And why shouldn't we be? We were standing there dripping wet from the rain, our clothes and hair drenched, and the sun was going down outside to cool the air even more.

I took another glance at the fireplace. And the little metal plaque on the wall beside it that I didn't remember being there before.

I stepped away from Arthur long enough to read the sign, then spun and gave him a wide grin.

"It's a gas fireplace. The damn thing actually works."

While I fiddled with the controls, trying to light the fireplace, Arthur hovered over me and begged me not to blow us up. When, with a solid *whump*, the flames ignited, shooting through the mound of phony ceramic logs, all cheery and bright and beautiful, he jumped in the air and clapped his hands like a Dallas cheerleader.

I laughed, took a minute to rub my hands in front of the warming flames, then turned to Arthur, and with what I hoped was a lecherous leer, growled, "Let's get those wet clothes off you before you catch your death."

He reached up to push my wet hair off my forehead. "Help me," he said sweetly, and at the gentle hunger in his voice, I felt my cock shift in anticipation.

"My God," I said. "You still do it to me."

"Do what?" he asked innocently, but by the wily look in his eyes, he knew exactly what I meant.

With trembling fingers, he began unbuttoning my shirt. When his thumb slid over my nipple, accidentally on purpose,

I began returning the favor, spreading his soaked shirt wide as I popped the buttons one by one. When the last button was released, I pushed the shirt from his shoulders, running my palms over his arms as I did. I leaned in to kiss the side of his neck, then stepped away to spread the shirt over a clotheshorse standing in the corner. After dragging the rack a little closer to the fire, Arthur again stepped into my arms until his warm chest was splayed sensuously over mine. He knelt before me and tugged off my shoes and socks. Then he unhooked my belt and pulled my slacks down to the floor and off my feet. When I was naked before him, he sat back on his haunches and gazed up at me.

Before he could act upon the ideas that were clearly going through his head, I pulled him to his feet and whispered, "My turn."

On my knees before *him*, I slipped off his shoes and socks, just as he had done for me, then snapped the button on his jeans, slid down the zipper, and watched in delight as his cock sprang out, fully erect, at the very moment his pants slid over his long legs and hit the floor.

I pressed my face to his thigh to smell the sweet scent of his skin. Before I could do anything else, he gently tugged me to my feet and led me toward the bathroom. "Let's shower," he said. "It's been a long day."

With my head on his shoulder and our two erect cocks bobbing and leading the way, we stepped into the old claw bathtub with the flowery shower curtain hanging around it. While Arthur bent to adjust the heat of the water, I stroked his sleek back and waited impatiently for him to rise up again and step into my arms.

When he had the water at a comfortable temperature, we stood face-to-face beneath the spray and slid our soapy hands over each other's skin.

"I still love the way you feel," he sputtered as he ducked his head into the downpour and pressed his mouth to mine. I trembled when he cupped my balls in his hand and stooped to kiss my chest. "Tell me you love me too, David."

"You know I do."

"Tell me anyway."

I pulled him tight against me, and this time it was my mouth that found his. Our tongues touched, and I thrilled at the way his hand slid from my balls and gently circled my cock instead. I rose up on tiptoes and buried my dick deeper in his fist. He smiled into our kiss when I did.

"You're such a slut," he muttered.

"Thank you," I muttered back, and his smile widened. "For an old dude, I try."

I slid my hands down his back until I felt the swell of his ass. When I dipped a finger in the crevice there, he too rose up on tiptoe and pressed himself closer to me.

"You like that," I said. "Now, don't lie. You know you do."

"Ass," he said.

"It most certainly is." I grinned. "A fine specimen indeed."

Arthur trembled in my arms as I rested a soapy fingertip on his opening and massaged the tender skin there gently. He pressed his face to my neck and mumbled, "We're clean enough. Take me to bed."

I nodded and turned off the shower. After snagging two towels off the rod, one for me and one for Arthur, we stood in the old claw-footed tub and dried each other off. Hand in hand, Arthur led me back to the only other room in the joint. It was warmer now. The fireplace was doing its job. Still, the bed was too far away from the heat.

"Help me," I said.

Before Arthur knew what was happening, I had pulled the mattress off the bed and dragged it to the floor in front of the flames. When Arthur realized what I was doing, he grabbed the pillows and the quilt and quickly arranged them over the mattress.

Satisfied, he sprawled naked at my feet on our newly arranged bed and stared up at me, his hands on my shins, his dick standing upright with no assistance from anybody.

"Lay with me," he whispered.

"Why?" I asked, teasing.

I stared down at him, and since he was staring up at me looking sexy as hell, I gave my engorged cock a stroke or two just to gauge his interest.

He didn't disappoint.

He rose to his knees and nuzzled his nose into my balls. At the feel of his warm tongue sliding between my legs, I laughed and barked, "You win!" and lowered myself to the mattress beside him. "And don't expect a premature ejaculation this time."

Arthur giggled. "Don't worry. I won't. AARP members almost *never* do that."

"Fuck you."

Still grinning, he scooped me into his arms, and we lay there with the heat of the gas flames warming our bodies. Our cocks lay hard, one against the other. Arthur's fingers were buried deep in my hair. His other hand caressed my hip, keeping me near.

His breath brushed my ear when he whispered softly, "Don't let me forget this moment, David. Whatever happens, make this the one moment I'll always remember. All right?"

I pulled away just far enough to look into his eyes. "Don't worry," I said, trying to ignore the burn of unwanted tears in my eyes. "I'll remember it for you, if that's what it takes. I'll remember and I'll remind you of it every chance I get. I love you, Arthur. We'll get through this."

"You mean tonight?"

"No. I mean we'll get through—*life*."

He dropped his head to my chest and nodded. I could feel his eyelashes tickling my skin. He brushed my nipple with his lips, and I cupped the back of his head to hold him in place.

"It could be years before it gets too bad," he said. "That's what you told me, right?"

I leaned down to press my lips to his hair. "Yes. That's what the doctor told *me*. Years and years. We'll still have a happy ending, Arthur."

He lifted his head and gazed at me with soulful eyes lit with hope. "We will, won't we? We're still together. We still excite each other."

I smiled and pulled his mouth back to my breast. "More than you know."

His arms circled my body, and I felt his fingertips trail down my spine. As I had done earlier, he slipped a finger into the fuzz between my asscheeks and headed south. When his fingers brushed my sphincter, I lifted a leg to give him better access. He didn't need an invitation to take full advantage of the opportunity.

"You're as beautiful as you were the day I met you."

"So are you, Arthur. Sometimes I think you're *more* beautiful."

"Do you feel old, David?"

"No," I answered truthfully. "Not like this. Not with you."

"Good," he muttered into my chest.

His mouth slid away from my nipple and began exploring the tender skin of my stomach, still heading south, always south.

"I'm sorry I haven't always been what you needed, Arthur. I'm sorry I couldn't be as good as you."

That stopped him. He raised himself onto one elbow and stared at me lying there beside him. He looked down at my cock, and with his thumb, he wiped away a rope of precome dangling from it. Bringing his thumb to his mouth, he kissed the precome away with a smile.

"It's not your fault, David. Time is the culprit, not you. Time makes us forget sometimes the things that are important. We get caught up in other pursuits, other—*fantasies.* But sooner or later we always come back to what's true, what's important."

"And what's that?" I asked, shuddering again as his hand returned to my cock and he buried it in his gentle grip.

"Us," he said. "That's the only thing that's really important. Us."

I brushed his pale hair from his forehead and smiled into his eyes. "Us," I whispered back.

He took a moment to slide his thumb across my lower lip, apparently just to savor the feel of it. When he was satisfied, he lifted my hand from his forehead and laid it on his stomach. "Touch me," he pleaded softly.

And since I couldn't bear to go another second without tasting this man I loved so much, I pushed him to his back and hovered over him, holding him in place. He watched with wide eyes, as I bent to kiss his chest, just as he had kissed mine. And as my mouth foraged over the familiar terrain of his stomach and into the even more familiar brush of strawberry-blond hair surrounding his straining cock, he caressed the back of my neck and held me there against him.

When I took his cock into my mouth, he lifted his hips and gently pleaded to be taken deeper. Just as I knew he would.

With eyes wide open, I swallowed his familiar girth and length and smiled as I felt him tremble beneath me.

My mind went back—back to the very first time I tasted the man.

Back to the beginning of our lifetime together....


HE SLEPT so peacefully beside me. After one coupling, his perfect body was still new to me. Still a mystery. He had shared it with me unhesitatingly, but the rush and heat of our lovemaking had left me blind to anything but senses, feelings. I knew the taste of him, but not really the sight. Blindfolded, I knew, I could pick out the feel of him from a hundred men. The silky heat of his skin was unforgettable. But my visual sense of him was still blunted. Unsatisfied.

To remedy that, I studied him as he lay sleeping beside me in the moonlight, his strong young legs splayed wide in sleep. Next to him, using his hip as my pillow, I thrilled even now to feel his cock, so hungry and eager before, warmly resting against my cheek. Unthreatening. Replete.

As he softly snored, his fingers lay woven through my hair. Being careful not to dislodge his tenuous hold on me, I eased my head from his hip and gazed up the long expanse of the man to his face. In sleep, there was an innocent smile on his lips that made my own lips twist into the very same mold.

The bedroom still smelled of our heated flesh, our exploded seed. Even now I could relive, resavor, the taste of his release. I could still feel the shattering explosion of my own release at the urging of his lips around my cock. The way he clutched me to him when I came. The way I didn't want to let him go, even as his cock softened in my mouth when we were through.

Gently, so as not to wake him, I softly tested the feel of the hair on his thigh, the hard sharp edges of his knee, the crisp lines of his ankle. I once again rested my cheek on his hip, letting the tickle of his pubic hair brush against my face. Pressing my lips even now to the soft rope of flesh nestled there, to feel its texture, to breathe in the scent of it. I began reading the man like braille. With feather-light strokes, I slid my fingertips over the sleek lines of his chest, the rubbery nubs of his nipples, that V-shaped indentation in his throat that still mesmerized me. Softly, oh so softly, I trailed my fingers down the line of his arm, the smooth economical bicep, the crook of his elbow where the hair and forearm began. It was there that I let my hand come to rest.

"Thank you," he whispered from the shadows above my head, and I realized for the first time that he wasn't asleep at all. His fingers moved in my hair. "What time is it?"

I had to seek out my voice. It had not been used since we made love. When I found it, oddly right where it always was, I whispered back, "It's not yet dawn, Arthur. Four o'clock, maybe. Or a little later. I'm sorry I woke you."

"Don't be," he breathed.

He curled over onto his side, pulling me into him, holding me in place, my face against his stomach, his strong hands caressing my shoulders, my neck, my hair.

He muttered something I couldn't quite understand in a voice I hardly recognized. He too was apparently battling to resurrect his voice from the place it had gone in sleep. He cleared his throat and said the same words again in a stronger, surer voice. "I love the way you feel."

I spoke my own words into his flesh, my lips against his skin. "Me too. You, I mean. The way *you* feel. Not me."

He didn't laugh but I could sense his smile in the darkness. He lifted his hand from my hair and pointed to the window above our heads. "Look at the moon, David. Look how big it is. I don't remember it being that big in England."

"I don't want to look at the moon," I said, my lips brushing his navel, the lazy thump of his heartbeat right there for me to hear and feel and conquer, as if it beat for me alone—as if I had ensnared it to be my own. "I only want to look at you."

He curled tighter around me, holding me close. We listened to each other breathe for a scatter of moments, then his voice eased through the darkness toward me. Toward me and through me.

"You know, David, the moon is like my heart, I think. Bigger than it usually is. It's almost as if you've filled it up. I'm surprised there's still room inside my heart for the blood to move through it with you in there taking up all the space."

I loved hearing the words, the lilt of his accent, the gentle way he expressed himself, but it was all still too new for me to voice my own thoughts on the subject, even if I could have admitted to myself what they truly were.

"We just met," I said. "We hardly know each other."

"I don't care," he said. "I still know you. I know everything I would ever need to know about you."

"Like what?" I asked. "What do you know? Tell me."

His cock was hardening against my cheek. I closed my eyes, stunned by the eroticism of feeling it there against me, lengthening, reaching out. The heat of it. The downy firmness of it. And I was stunned too by his words. By the confident way he spoke them. The assuredness of them.

"I know you're kind. I know you're sweet. I know you make love the same way I do. With every sensation, every breath, every hunger guiding you through the motions. Taking you where you want to go. Refusing to be denied. When you make love, and afterwards, like now, you want it all, David. You want to enjoy every moment as deeply as you can."

I wasn't sure why, but I knew I needed to dilute his words. Water them down. It scared me to think where they might take us if I didn't. "I guess that makes me a cuddler," I said.

"Yes," he smiled down at me as if he knew what I was up to. "A cuddler, if that's how you want to think of it."

I felt my eyelashes brush his stomach as I considered his words. Even as his cock pressed more insistently against my cheek, making my own cock waken and lengthen and stretch itself out as far as it could go, I tried to focus on the things he'd said. The words he'd used.

And the inescapable truth of them.

"I've never been with anyone like you," I said, still smiling at the feel of his dick growing impossibly harder with the movement of my lips brushing against it. "I don't know what it is. Even before we did the things we did tonight, there was something about you, sitting there on that bench in the mission garden that took my breath away. And now, Arthur, now that I've known you—*completely*—I don't know what to make of it. What to make—of you."

"Don't ever think you know me completely," he said. The words sounded sad coming from his lips.

"I'm sorry. I didn't mean—"

But he wouldn't let me finish. "Make whatever you want of me, David. Make me be what you want me to be."

"But I don't know what that is."

"Not yet, maybe," he said, wiggling down in the bed until his face was directly in line with mine, his fingers still buried in my hair. I stared into his handsome young face, and in the shadowy moonlight, his azure eyes were almost colorless. Riveting. They were the most beautiful eyes I had ever seen. It all but took my breath away to see them now focused so unerringly, so unhesitatingly, on me and me alone.

He sweetly tasted my mouth with his lips. He gently nipped at my lower lip with his teeth. And while I didn't want to lose sight of those pale, heavenly eyes, I finally couldn't help myself. I closed my own, blocking out the sight of him, and let the taste and feel of his kiss fill my thoughts instead.

"Mmmm," he breathed against me. "You're better than cake."

I couldn't help myself. I laughed.

He lifted his mouth from mine and stared into my eyes, just as before I had stared into his. He was smiling broadly, his hair a tangled mess around his face. He was so heartstoppingly beautiful, I wanted to freeze the moment for all eternity and just lie there looking at him. Forever.

Then I laughed again. This time at myself. *Who knew I could ever be so goddamn smitten? And after one night. One measly night.*

"Yes," he beamed, his eyes bright and shimmering in the moonlight. "Laugh for me. I love it when you laugh."

And moments later, as our hunger for each other took over completely, even my laughter couldn't hold his attention.

Forty years later, in the middle of a rainstorm, I would finally understand.


THE FLAMES cast flickering shadows around the room. We lay in each other's arms on the mattress in front of the fireplace, our bodies damp with sweat now, instead of rain. I could still taste Arthur's come on my tongue.

"I understand it now," I said, my lips against the side of his neck.

He nuzzled closer, burying his face in my hair. "Understand what, David?"

"I understand that I loved you then."

"Then when?"

"Then," I said. "On that very first night we were together. Here. In this very room. Forty years ago."

Arthur held me tightly for a few seconds. Then I began to feel a tremor in his body. I pulled far enough away to see his face and realized he was quietly chuckling. I bit back a teeny surge of anger.

"What the hell are you laughing at?"

"You," he said. "I'm laughing at you."

"But why?"

"Because it didn't take me four decades to figure that out. I figured it out that very night. I knew we loved each other *then*. On that very first night, I knew we would always be together."

"Did you?"

"Yes."

I hesitated, but finally had to ask the question foremost in my mind. "Do you really remember that night, Arthur? Do you honestly remember it the way I do? Was it—was it as magical for you as it was for me?"

He again tucked himself against me and pulled me close. "Yes, David. The dementia hasn't taken that away from me yet. And if it ever does, I figure the memories will still live on anyway. They'll live on inside of you. You'll store them for me, won't you? You'll tend them like roses until we find each other again on the other side of whatever comes after."

"Yes," I said. "I'll store them for you. I'll keep them safe. Every memory. Every word we shared. Every touch. That night and every night we've lain in each other's arms since. I'll keep them all safe and sound for you, Arthur, I promise, just in case you ever need them."

"Good." He whispered the word softly as he lifted his head and closed his eyes as if enjoying the heat of the flames on his face. "Good."

Still in each other's arms, we stretched out before the fire like a couple of cats, savoring the heat, savoring the feel of each other's bodies.

Off in the distance, I heard the rain still pummeling the porch roof. Even farther off, somewhere out across the ocean swells, a faint boom of thunder stirred the night.

Softly, beside me, Arthur asked in a sleepy voice, "I wonder where they went."

I tore my attention from the storm outside the room and returned it to the man beside me—the man who would always be beside me.

"What are you talking about, Arthur? Where did *who* go?"

"The swallows," he said. The words were spoken so softly they barely stirred the air around us. Pensive. Pondering. "At the mission. It was sad not seeing them there. I was just wondering—where they went."

He nestled closer to me as I considered his words. He was right, of course. The old mission had seemed incomplete without the swallows singing and stirring among the eaves, sweeping over the gardens.

I studied Arthur's face in the flickering firelight, his head only inches from mine as we shared the same pillow, our arms still holding each other tight. Arthur's hair, once damp from the shower, had dried during the throes of passion, and now it stuck out all over the place like a field of sunbaked brambles. I smiled and tried to pat it back in place. I don't know why. My own hair probably looked worse than his.

Before I could think of an answer to what he'd said, I saw his eyelids begin to droop. His face relaxed as it always did when he fell into sleep.

I held my breath, watching him. The gray in his hair looked blond again in the firelight. The reflection of orange flames smoothed the age lines in his face, which even I had to admit there were fewer of than on my own. In the dim, flickering light, he looked as young as he had the first day I held him in my arms, forty years before. And oddly enough, he still felt and tasted the same. He was more familiar to me now; in fact, I think I knew his body better than I knew my own. But familiarity had not lessened my desire for him. It hadn't lessened it one iota.

I longed to stroke the stubble on his cheek (we both needed a shave and would look like hobos by morning), but I didn't want to disturb his tumble into sleep, his gentle retreat from the day.

Just before he closed his eyes and let sleep take him completely, he mumbled two words. And as he mumbled them, the warmth of his breath touched my face.

"Poor swallows," he said.

And I waited silently in his arms as his breathing steadied and his body relaxed into total sleep.
*Poor swallows indeed.*

NAKED, I sat in the window seat by the front door and stared out at the rain and intermittent flashes of lightning in the distance. The room was warm now from the flames in the fireplace, although I probably would have been naked anyway since our clothes were still wet and steaming on the clotheshorse by the fire. Idly I wondered if they would even be dry by morning.

The sound of Arthur's breathing softly stirred the darkness in the room. I longed to crawl back onto the mattress with him and fold him into my arms in the heat of the flames, but there was something I had to do first. A debt I had to repay. A debt long outstanding.

I gazed down at the sheets of stationery I had quietly scavenged from a drawer in the bureau beneath the minibar. The B&B even provided me with a pen. I used a phone book, which I found in the same drawer, as a makeshift lap desk.

In the illumination of the porch light streaming through the window, I began to write my long-promised love letter to Arthur. And as I wrote, I began to realize all the things I hadn't said over the years. All the things that should have been said, not once, but time and time again. Arthur had a romantic soul. He would have cherished words of love now and then. Out of the blue, maybe. Not just when we were having sex when the words seemed to come more naturally, more easily. But during breakfast, or as we walked, or while we cleaned the house, or when we were rushing out the door to go to work, back in the days when work controlled our lives. How much effort does it take to stop a person in the course of an average day and simply tell them how much you love them? How much they mean to you?

Squinting into the dim light, I again touched pen to paper and watched the pages fill. The words poured out. Without thought, seemingly. They were so long overdue it was as if they had been eagerly trembling there forever, just inside my head, waiting for me to finally open the floodgates and set them free.

My feelings for Arthur. All he meant to me. While I knew now that I had loved him from the beginning, how sorry I was to have never given him the *attention* he deserved. The *devotion*. How stupid I had been not to realize that sometimes love isn't quite enough. Sometimes a person needs the words that go with it. No, not sometimes. Always. They *always* need the words.

I blamed it on age, of course. Old fucking age. The way I had let the years slip by and how not truly worshipping Arthur had grown easier and easier as our youth receded. Like Arthur had said, it was time that was the culprit. Time and the ennui that comes with it. But was that really true? Even in our youth, my eyes had wandered. My eyes and my imagination. While I hadn't truly cheated—except for that one time at Yosemite, that much was true—I had still been remiss in not giving Arthur all he deserved from a lover, and later, when it became legal to marry, all he needed from a husband.

While I had carried my love for Arthur all but hidden inside myself all those years we were together, I could not understand now why I hadn't let him know about it more often.

Only now, now that our long years together were drawing to a close, thanks to the goddamn dementia, I couldn't wait another minute to tell him or it would be too late. Before he would wake one morning and perhaps not be capable of understanding love at all.

Sitting there in the shadows, listening to the fall of rain and the gentle thrum of Arthur softly snoring behind me, words flowed onto the paper just as raindrops flowed down the pane of glass in front of me.

I wrote and wrote and wrote. Only when my fingers began to cramp did I stop and fold the pages neatly and slip them into one of the green envelopes with the bed-and-breakfast's logo on the front. Sealing it closed with the tip of my tongue, I laid the envelope on the windowsill and turned my attention to the mattress in front of the fire.

I was exhausted. Slipping under the warm blanket, I eased my arm over Arthur's chest and rested my head on the pillow beside his head.

Before I slid into weary sleep, I felt him turn to me and cuddle close, not once opening his eyes or tearing himself awake.

I lay there in the arms of the man I had loved since the moment I met him, almost a lifetime ago, and the last thing I remember before sleep finally took me was the feel of a cool tear sliding over the bridge of my nose and splattering the pillow between our heads.

*How long will I have him?* I asked myself. *How long will he know he is mine?*

As always, as I slept, my dreams were full of the man beside me.


WHEN I opened my eyes, the room was flooded with light. I could tell by the feel and scent of the air around me that early morning had slipped away. Hunger pangs brought me *fully* awake when I realized I smelled coffee and pastry somewhere close by.

I sat up on the mattress and looked around the rented room just as Arthur turned and gazed at me from the window seat where I had sat the night before. Behind Arthur's head, the morning shone gray and drear through the windowpane, but at least the rain had stopped. The storm was over.

Arthur was wrapped in a sheet from the bed, his strong legs peering through, his shoulders pale and perfect in the morning light. In Arthur's hands and in his lap, he held the scattered pages of the letter I had written in the middle of the night.

He saw where I was looking and sheepishly batted his eyes. Playfully, I think. At least I hoped so.

"The envelope had my name on it, so I opened it. That's all right, isn't it?"

I nodded. "Yes. Of course. I—I wrote it for you."

"It's my love letter, isn't it?"

"Yes, Arthur. Somehow, after last night, being with you here on this bed in front of this fire, I couldn't seem *not* to write it. The words just kind of spilled out of me. Were you able to read my writing? My penmanship sucks."

He smiled gently. "Your penmanship was fine. And yes, love. I read it all. Twice. Thank you."

I slid from beneath the quilt and naked, sporting morning wood, I knee-walked quickly toward the window seat where he sat. Squatting on the floor before him, I wrapped my arms around his waist and pulled him to me. With my face buried in his stomach, I mumbled the words I should have said so many times before, but never seemed to manage.

"I love you, Arthur. I've never loved anyone more than I love you. I love the way you never let me slip away, even when I was being a dick. I love the way you stood by me when I was cold to you, or mean, or just plain asshole-y. I even love the way you gave me all the room in the world to make a complete ass of myself, but still never bitched about me being a twit. I've never deserved you, but you even overlooked that and committed yourself to me anyway." I lifted my face from his lap and closed my eyes as his soft fingers stroked my cheek. I spoke to the darkness behind my eyelids because I was too ashamed to speak the words in light to Arthur's face. "As long as I have you, I have everything I need, Arthur. I've always known it, but now it's time you knew it too. I'm sorry. Please forgive me."

"And your fantasies?" he asked gently. "What about those?"

I swallowed my guilt, buoyed by the love I still saw in his eyes. He hadn't forsaken me. I suppose I always knew he never would. "From this day forward," I said, "my fantasies are all of you. In truth, I think they always were."

"I know, David. I think I always knew."

His fingers caressed my ear as he gazed down at me. He tucked my lobe between his thumb and forefinger as if mesmerized by the texture of it. The stubble on my cheek scraped the back of his hand, and he seemed mesmerized by that too, pressing his hand a little harder against my face as if he couldn't quite seem to get enough.

I finally took a breath of air, not realizing until that instant that I had been holding it in fear. Fear of what Arthur might say, what Arthur might do. But I should have known better. To my infinite relief, I watched him smile down at me. A lone tear lay balanced on a blond lash, and as I watched, it trembled for a moment, then fell, skimming downward to the corner of his mouth. I watched in wonder as he licked it away.

"I'm sorry," I said, twisting my head to kiss his palm. "I'm so sorry, Arthur."

He smiled down at me, and the smile wiped every year, every pain, from his face. And from my own as well. "Never be sorry for who you are," he said quietly. "Not with me. And don't be sorry for the things you think you've done either. I know you better than you do. We might have pulled apart at times over the years, but we never came close to separating completely. Not once. I knew you loved me, David, even when you maybe thought you didn't." He coughed up a wry chuckle. "And I can be a dick too. I just haven't perfected it as well as you."

I laughed and he wrapped his sheet around me so that my face could lie against his bare skin. I kissed his stomach and felt his rising cock nudge my chin.

In the diffused light beneath the sheet, I felt myself still smiling. The scent of him was so wonderful I gave a teeny shudder of lust. I wrapped my arms around his bare back and kissed his thigh, his hip, his stomach.

"I'd kill for a toothbrush," I said.

He pulled a paper bag from behind his back and rattled it in front of my face.

"What's that?" I asked.

"Toothbrushes, toothpaste, deodorant, and a roll of floss. I found an all-night drugstore open down the street."

"You snuck out in the middle of the night?"

"Nope, this morning while you were snoring like a drunken sailor."

"They didn't have hair spray?"

"Oh, shut up."

Then I muttered, "Do I smell doughnuts on your breath?"

"They had those too."

"Do you know how hungry I am?"

"I left you some. There's coffee too."

"Oh my God, you're an angel."

He laid his hand over the nape of my neck, and with his other hand, he used a fingertip to tap my head like he might have tapped a watermelon in the supermarket to test its ripeness. "If I feed you and give you coffee, can we have a quick fuck before we check out?"

"Oh, Arthur. You should know by now. For coffee and doughnuts, I'd fuck a walrus."


ARTHUR HELD me in his strong arms. My teeth were still clamped to his bicep, the same place they had migrated to when he came. Both of us were trembling and damp with sweat. Slowly, oh so slowly, his cock softened deep inside me. "There," he said huskily into my ear. "Now you're fucked."

I couldn't speak. All I could do was nod. *And fucked well*, I thought. *Fucked extremely well.*

Arthur held me tight, his free hand still holding my come-soaked dick. "Let me lick it away," he said. "Like I did that first time we stood naked in this room. The time you couldn't restrain yourself, remember?"

"Don't you dare pull away from me. I want to feel you inside me a while longer. Please, Arthur. Don't move."

He nuzzled the back of my neck, kissing me there, breathing his sweet breath over me. His warm stomach lay flat against my back, the front of his thighs against the back of my own. The blond hair on his forearm felt glorious against my chin, and I still relished the taste of him on my lips. I reached around behind me to urge him deeper. He eased his hips closer, trying to give me what I wanted.

"All right," he hushed, soothing me like a child. "All right."

We lay like that for the longest time. I was just beginning to doze when I felt Arthur's cock, fully flaccid now, finally slip away from me. I sighed, missing it already. And just as I sighed, I felt Arthur grow tense against me. His body stiffened. Everything but his dick, that is, which in my opinion was a fucking shame.

I twisted my head to the side to try to see what had grabbed his attention. "What is it? What's wrong?"

He pointed to the window. "Look," he said in a hushed whisper. "Look there."

I aimed my gaze at the spot where he was pointing and saw a bird perched on the windowsill. A tiny bird. He was preening and smoothing his feathers as if attending to his morning ablutions. The bird's delicate wings were dark brown, his breast white. A high collar of burnt orange circled his throat and just above his darting eyes and short beak, sat a triangle of white feathers, giving him a solemn, determined appearance as if every ounce of his concentration was centered on the job at hand. At intervals he would stop preening and study his reflection in the glass, cocking his tiny head first one way then the other. Once, he pecked at the windowpane, and the startled look on his face when he realized it wasn't another bird in front of him made us laugh out loud.

Arthur was so excited he trembled against me. I felt his mouth moving against my scalp as he uttered his words into my hair. I could imagine him peering over the top of my head, as bright-eyed and rapt as the bird studying its own reflection. "It's a swallow, David! It's a mission swallow!"

I nodded, mute with wonder, as Arthur's heart thundered against my back.


"THE BOY at the bed and breakfast said it's right around here."

"He had a crucifix in his ear," Arthur said. "He's liable to say anything."

"I know, but stop sounding like an old poop and try to keep your mind on the big picture."

Arthur chuckled, and together we dug our bare toes into the sand as we traipsed down the beach. There were no sunbathers out because there was also no sun. The sky was still full of leftover storm clouds from the night before. There was a nip in the air that smelled of boggy earth and rain-washed foliage. While the beach was empty of humanity, except for us, out across the gray swells, we spotted two surfers, both in wet suits, sprawled across their boards, braving pneumonia in hopes a decent wave would come along and give them their first high of the day.

Since there was no one else nearby, Arthur took my hand. Our other hands were filled with shoes and socks.

"We have two hours before the train comes."

"I know, Arthur. You've told me a dozen times."

"Have I?" He seemed surprised.

"Yes, but that's okay," I quickly said. "I need reminding."

"Oh. Well, then, it's all right that I'm annoying."

"Yes. *More* than all right, in fact. I've come to expect it and rely on it. Your ability to annoy is what keeps me functioning."

He giggled and mumbled, "Horseshit."

Up ahead, just a few yards inland from the beach, a crevasse in the coastline opened up. We were perhaps a mile from the town of San Juan Capistrano. There were still beach houses scattered about, and on the other side of the houses, we could hear traffic motoring back and forth along the freeway. Running parallel to the freeway, we knew, lay the train tracks that would later carry us home.

But first we had a job to do.

"This must be the place," I said, steering us off the sand and into a tangle of bracken and wind-stunted arroyo willows. Before we left the beach entirely, we sat in the damp sand and redonned our shoes and socks.

"Do you really think they're here?" Arthur asked softly, his voice filled with hope.

I shrugged. "That's what he said."

Shod, we ducked through the mouth of the gulley. The arroyo willows, standing tall and billowy, shaded us from the sky, and the ground beneath our feet became uneven and rocky. On any other day of the year, I could imagine the gulley being dusty and sunbaked, but after the storm of the night before, the ground was squishy and soft. The hum of bees buzzing in the thickets, perhaps lapping at the rain-washed petals of wild flowers, filled the air around us.

"This is like an adventure. It's exciting," Arthur said, once again taking my hand and cautiously leading me around a puddle as if I didn't have enough sense to sidestep it myself.

I laughed. "You're sense of excitement has grown goofy of late."

He smiled, and I gripped his hand a little tighter, pulling him to a stop.

"Let me kiss that," I said.

"Kiss what?" he asked, but I could tell he already knew.

"Your smile."

He blushed. "All right," he said.

So I did. Standing there in the shadows among the scrub and sage and rocky ravine walls, we might have been the only two humans on the planet. Two old remnants of a world gone by. But at the moment, age was the last thing on my mind. Arthur's kiss still tasted sweet from the toothpaste he had picked up at the all-night drugstore. I hoped mine did too. With his arms around me, I felt anchored to the ground beneath me. Anchored to the life I was living. The bright gleam of happiness in his eyes as our lips met made my heart beat a happy little staccato rhythm inside my chest.

In the distance I could still hear the drone of automobiles on the freeway somewhere up ahead. That sound brought me back to the business at hand. After I broke the kiss, Arthur continued to hold me fast against him. "Don't let me forget this, David. None of it. You promised."

"Never, my love. Now come on. Time is running out."

I once again took his hand and led him deeper into the arroyo. As we stumbled over the rocks and through the bracken, the sound of traffic grew louder. Then I noticed stone abutments where a steel trestle stretched across the canyon.

Then we heard it again. The gentle thrum of automobiles, and suddenly—*birds*.

And with that first hint of birdsong, Arthur took the lead. Clutching hands, we threaded our way through the bracken and sage and over the rocks, stumbling now, because the ground was so uneven and our legs were not as young as they had once been. We passed into the shade of the train trestle and there, among the shadows, Arthur dragged me to a stop.

"Look," he whispered. "Up there. Among the beams."

I squinted to see what Arthur was pointing at. And then I saw them. Clustered among the eaves of the trestle, in every nook, on every surface. Nests. Hundreds and hundreds of nests. Mud-walled, with perfectly round openings in the front like teeny hobbit doors. The nests looked almost like wasp nests, I thought. They were so uniform in size and shape, and every one of them so perfectly matched the others they might have been stamped from a machine.

"Swallows' nests," Arthur whispered excitedly.

"Are you sure?"

"Yes. Look at all of them!"

Suddenly another sound inserted itself in the background. A rumbling, throaty roar. Loud. And growing louder by the second.

It was a train. An Amtrak. We could hear the rattle and clank of the tracks beneath it as the train approached from the south. Not our train. Another. Headed in the opposite direction. Through gaps in the arroyo willows, I could see it. I caught flashes of light, glimpses of shining metal, the reflection of cloudy sky on wide windowpanes, the blue-and-red arrow streak of an Amtrak logo, all drawing near. Moving up the coast. Headed straight for us.

A second later the train was upon us in an avalanche of noise. The unearthly clanking of wheel on rail froze us in our tracks. Tons of metal sliding over our heads shook the very ground beneath our feet, rendering us speechless. Dust sifted down upon us.

And the moment the sound of the train surrounded us completely, numbing us, or so one would suppose, to all other sounds, another sound filled the air. A sharper sound.

A *living* sound.

And a heartbeat later, there they were. The swallows. In a thudding whirr of wings and bodies, they exploded from their mud nests, thousands of them, disturbed by the train, sweeping first this way, then that, filling the air with their raucous cries. Their song was so strident, so piercing, Arthur and I clapped our hands to our ears, laughing and cringing at the same time. More than once I felt the breath of wings flapping past my face and rustling my hair. I watched Arthur, still laughing, holding his hand high in the air like a tree branch hoping a swallow would land on it, just to say hello, to acknowledge his presence.

Between the scream of the train and the cries of the birds, speech was impossible. Arthur and I stood there, shoulder to shoulder, each as stunned as the other by the beauty of that whirling storm of birds. Gradually, as the train slid past overhead and the last cars rattled away in the distance, we were left with just the sound of the swallows. Diving. Swooping. Still screaming their outraged cries to high heaven. Hundreds of them. Thousands. Darting this way and that, en masse, shifting black to white to black as they wheeled around our heads, pinioning, veering left and right and in great sweeping circles.

And then slowly, as their startled songs began to quiet, they returned to their nests, one by one. The sky around our heads emptied out as the birds somehow found their respective homes, and their respective young, which we could now also hear, cheeping sweetly and insistently inside their shadowed houses of mud and twig.

As the last few swallows returned to their nests through their little hobbit doors, Arthur once again reached out and took my hand. He was trembling from head to foot with excitement, his smile as broad as I had ever seen it.

"We can go home now," he said, and immediately, for the briefest of moments I saw doubt cross his face. He appeared suddenly lost. A shadow of indecision and yes, for a split second, fear widened his eyes.

I slid the back of my fingers gently over his stubbly cheek and, with a shushing sound, said, "Don't worry, Arthur. I know where it is."

His smile returned as quickly as it left. He leaned his head into the touch of my fingers. "Then everything's all right."

"Yes," I said. "As right as rain."

LATER, ON the train headed south, he sat beside me, content and happy—just as content and happy as I was to have him there. At my side. Leading me through life. And for a good while longer, I hoped. Years, if God was kind. Years and years.

In his hand Arthur clutched the love letter I had written back at the inn.

He read the letter over and over as the silent, swaying train carried us toward our home. And all the time he read, his other hand never left mine.

Once, as we stared out at the setting sun sinking below the rim of the ocean, he turned to me and asked, "Any fantasies going on in that twisted mind of yours?"

I gave him my very best evil smirk. "Only one," I said.

"What is it?"

"Follow me to the bathroom, and I'll explain it in detail."

He laughed. And when he was finished laughing, he tucked my love letter in his pocket and stepped out into the aisle.

With a wink, he leaned in and whispered, "I'll meet you there."

JOHN INMAN has been writing fiction since he was old enough to hold a pencil. He and his partner live in beautiful San Diego, California. Together, they share a passion for theater, books, hiking and biking along the trails and canyons of San Diego or, if the mood strikes, simply kicking back with a beer and a movie. John's advice for anyone who wishes to be a writer? "Set time aside to write every day and do it. Don't be afraid to share what you've written. Feedback is important. When a rejection slip comes in, just tear it up and try again. Keep mailing stuff out. Keep writing and rewriting and then rewrite one more time. Every minute of the struggle is worth it in the end, so don't give up. Ever. Remember that publishers are a lot like lovers. Sometimes you have to look a long time to find the one that's right for you."

E-mail: john492@att.net
Facebook: http://www.facebook.com/john.inman.79
Website: http://www.johninmanauthor.com/

# *Head-on*

By John Inman

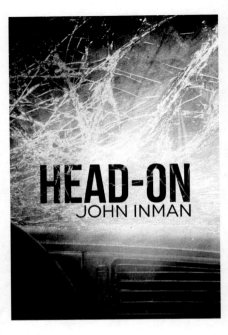

At twenty-six, Gordon Stafford figures his days are numbered. At least he hopes they are. Wearied by guilt and regret stemming from a horrific automobile accident two years earlier in which a man was killed, Gordon wakes up every morning with thoughts of suicide. While the law puts Gordon to work atoning for his sins, personal redemption is far harder to come by.

Then Squirt—a simple homeless man with his own crosses to bear—saves Gordon from a terrible fate. Overnight, Gordon finds not only a new light to follow, and maybe even a purpose to his life, but also the possibility of love waiting at the end of the tunnel.

Gordon never imagined he'd discover a way to forgive himself, and in doing so, open his heart enough to gain acceptance and love—from the very person he hurt the most.

# *Hobbled*

By John Inman

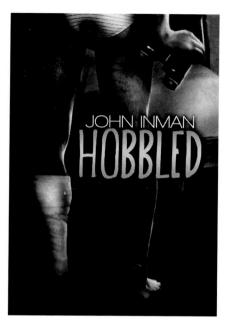

Thanks to fate and his own lack of good sense, eighteen-year-old Danny Shay is headed into what looks to be the worst summer of his life. It starts with a minor meltdown at work that leaves Danny under house arrest with a cast on one leg and an ankle monitor on the other, courtesy of the San Diego Police Department. On top of that, he's battling a chronic case of virginity, with no relief in sight.

Oh, and there's one more little glitch. A serial killer is stalking the city, murdering young men. And when strange sounds are heard in the house behind Danny's, the neighborhood kids think they've found the killer. But not until Danny learns he's next on the madman's list do things *really* begin to get desperate.

Damn! And Danny had plans to come out this summer—maybe even get laid! He doesn't have *time* for ankle monitors and serial killers!

Then ginger-haired Luke Jamison moves in next door. Not only does Luke solve a few of Danny's more *urgent* problems, he also manages to create a couple more that Danny never saw coming. Gee. If he can survive it, this summer might not be so bad after all.

# http://www.dreamspinnerpress.com

# Jasper's Mountain

By John Inman

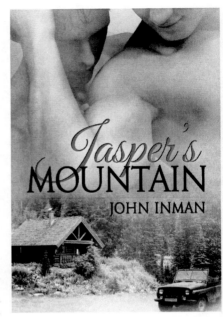

When small-time thief Timmy Harwell recklessly "borrows" a Cadillac for a joyride, he doesn't expect to find a cool $100,000 in the trunk. His elation turns to terror when he realizes the SUV and the dough belong to Miguel Garcia, aka El Poco, a Tijuana drug dealer with a nasty reputation. Timmy sees only one way out: leave the stolen car behind and run as fast as he can.

His getaway is cut short when a storm strands him outside Jasper Stone's secluded mountain cabin. Jasper finds Timmy in his shed, unconscious and burning up with fever, and takes care of the younger man, nursing him back to health. The two begin to grow close, but Jasper, a writer who seeks only solitude, is everything Timmy isn't. Straightforward, honest, and kind.

Timmy needs Jasper's help—and wants his respect—so he hides his dishonest habits. But when El Poco comes after him, Timmy realizes he's not the only one at risk. His actions have also put Jasper in harm's way. Honesty now could mean Timmy loses the man he's come to love, but not being honest could mean far worse.

## http://www.dreamspinnerpress.com

# *Loving Hector*

By John Inman

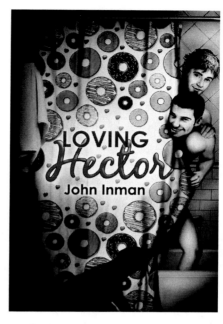

Dillard Brown has a mother who's determined he's straight, a writing career that's going nowhere, and at thirty, he's never been in love in his life. But thanks to a ten-pound ball of fluff and energy named Chester, one of Dill's circumstances is about to change. Maybe even all three.

Who would've thought one little stray dog could change Dill's world—and not by accident either. The damn dog has it planned. If not for Chester wandering into Dill's life and into his heart, Dill would never have met Hector Peña—and tumbled headlong into love at last!

But for all Chester's efforts, happiness for Dill and Hector is still not assured. Hector's evil ex, Valdemaro, is dead set on holding on—even if it means kidnapping Hector to keep him from Dill forever! Now Dill has to pull an army together to rescue Hector, and just where the hell is he supposed to find an army? Gads, if only Dill could write books this interesting!

# http://www.dreamspinnerpress.com

# *Paulie*

## By John Inman

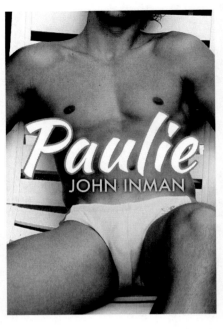

To the casual observer, Paulie Banks lives the perfect life. After all, he's young, handsome, and rich. But Paulie has a secret. He's madly in love with Ben, his old college roommate—and Ben is straight! Now Paulie has arranged a two-week reunion with his three closest friends to rehash their college years and get to know each other again. Jamie and Trevor are coming, along with their new lovers. And to Paulie's amazement, even Ben has accepted his invitation.

Beautiful Ben. The one non-gay apple in the old college barrel. Paulie will soon find out if Ben has forgiven him for overstepping the bounds of friendship on the last drunken night they spent together.

With his La Jolla mansion spotless, a stunning new houseboy hired for the duration, and his heart pounding in both fear and anticipation, Paulie welcomes his old friends back into his life. Thanks to a whole lot of liquor and a clothing-optional dress code, boy, do the festivities begin!

# http://www.dreamspinnerpress.com

# *Payback*

### By John Inman

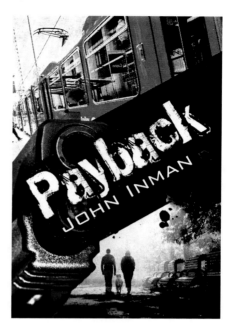

When Tyler Powell's life is torn apart by an unspeakable crime, the need for vengeance takes over. Every moment of every day, as he tries to pull his shattered existence together again, it's all he can think about—revenge.

Will he give in to his rage and become the very thing he hates most? A killer?

Only with the help of Homicide Detective Christian Martin, the cop in charge of his case, does Tyler see the possibility of another life beginning—the astounding revelation of another love reaching out to him. A love he thought he would never know again.

Will he let that love into his life, or is he lost already? Is payback more important to Tyler than his own happiness? And the happiness of the man who loves him? Tyler is determined to find a way to exact his revenge without sacrificing all hope for a future with Christian, but it will be difficult—if not impossible—and in the end he might be forced to make an unbearable choice.

# http://www.dreamspinnerpress.com

# The Poodle Apocalypse

By John Inman

With the world suddenly teeming with zombies, Charlie and Bobby are fighting to stay alive. Being about as gay as two people can be, they insist on doing it with panache.

Even with the planet throwing up its legs in submission, there is no reason a couple of style-conscious guys can't look good while saying good-bye to the age of man and ushering in the age of… God knows what. Amoebas, maybe. With their loyal zombie poodle, Mimi, at their side, they bravely face the apocalypse head-on.

Death, destruction, and the undead they can deal with. But without electricity, it's the depressing lack of blow-dryers and cappuccino machines that really pisses them off—until Bobby goes missing! Suddenly Charlie has more than fluffy hair and a good cup of coffee to worry about….

## http://www.dreamspinnerpress.com

# *Spirit*

## By John Inman

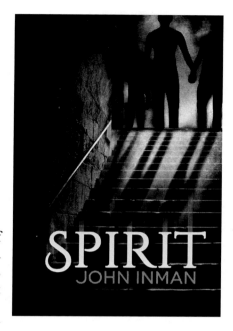

Jason Day, brilliant designer of video games, is not only a confirmed bachelor, but he's as gay as a maypole. One wouldn't think being saddled with his precocious four-year-old nephew for four weeks would be enough to throw him off-kilter.

Wrong. Timmy, Jason's nephew, is a true handful.

But just when Timmy and Uncle Jason begin to bond, and Jason feels he's getting a grip on this babysitting business once and for all, he's thrown for a loop by a couple of visitors—one from Tucson, the other from beyond the grave.

I'm sorry. Say what?

Toss a murder, a hot young stud, an unexpected love affair, and a spooky-ass ghost with a weird sense of humor into Jason's summer plans, and you've got the makings for one hell of a ride.

# http://www.dreamspinnerpress.com

# *Serenading Stanley*

## A Belladonna Arms Novel

### By John Inman

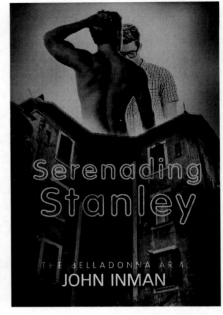

Welcome to the Belladonna Arms, a rundown little apartment building perched atop a hill in downtown San Diego, home to the city's lost and lovelorn. Shy archaeology student Stanley Sternbaum has just moved in and fills his time quietly observing his eccentric neighbors, avoiding his hellion mother, and trying his best to go unnoticed… which proves to be a problem when it comes to fellow tenant Roger Jane. Smitten, the hunky nurse with beautiful green eyes does everything in his power to woo Stanley, but Stanley has always lived a quiet life, too withdrawn from the world to take a chance on love. Especially with someone as beautiful as Roger Jane.

While Roger tries to batter down Stanley's defenses, Stanley turns to his new neighbors to learn about love: Ramon, who's not afraid to give his heart to the wrong man; Sylvia, the trans who just wants to be a woman, and the secret admirer who loves her just the way she is; Arthur, the aging drag queen who loves them all, expecting nothing in return—and Roger, who has been hurt once before but is still willing to risk his heart on Stanley, if Stanley will only look past his own insecurities and let him in.

# http://www.dreamspinnerpress.com

# *Work in Progress*

## A Belladonna Arms Novel

### By John Inman

Dumped by his lover, Harlie Rose ducks for cover in the Belladonna Arms, a seedy apartment building perched high on a hill in downtown San Diego. What he doesn't know is that the Belladonna Arms has a reputation for romance—and Harlie is about to become its next victim.

Finding a job at a deli up the street, Harlie meets Milan, a gorgeous but cranky baker. Unaware that Milan is suffering the effects of a broken heart just as Harlie is, the two men circle around each other, manning the barricades, both unwilling to open themselves up to love yet again.

But even the most stubborn heart can be conquered.

With his new friends to back him up—Sylvia, on the verge of her final surgery to become a woman, Arthur, the aging drag queen who is about to discover a romance of his own, and Stanley and Roger, the handsome young couple in 5C who lead by example, Harlie soon learns that at the Belladonna Arms, love is always just around the corner waiting to pounce. Whether you want it to or not.

But tragedy also drops in now and then.

## http://www.dreamspinnerpress.com

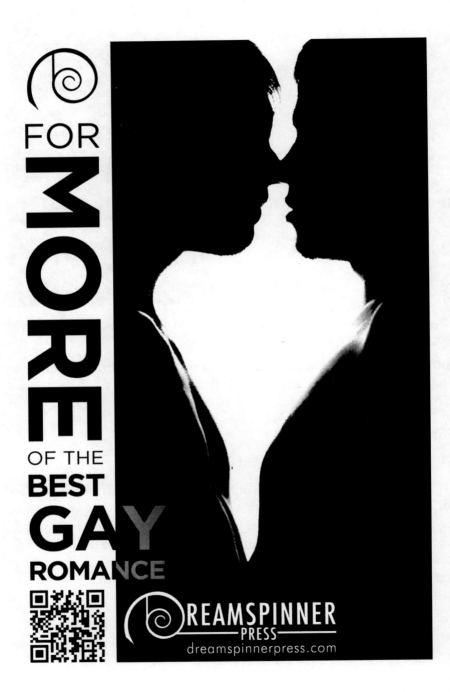

Manufactured by Amazon.ca
Acheson, AB